"Did you ever intend telling me?"

"It's none of your business," Georgina said stubbornly.

"My child is none of my business?" His blue eyes glittered ferociously.

"Biologically you're the father," she admitted hoarsely. "But your part was over a long time ago. What we had was casual; a brief moment of madness."

Callum's head jerked as though she'd struck him. "You can't really think I'm willing to let you deny me contact with my child?"

"I want this child and you're not going to take him from me!"

KIM LAWRENCE lives on a farm in rural Anglesey, Wales. She runs two miles daily and finds this an excellent opportunity to unwind and seek inspiration for her writing. It also helps her keep up with her husband, two active sons and the various stray animals that have adopted them. Always a fanatical consumer of fiction, she is now equally enthusiastic about writing. She loves a happy ending!

Kim Lawrence is a bright new talent in Harlequin Presents®. She loves creating strong, sexy heroes and spirited, lively heroines to tame them!

Look out for future books by Kim in Presents™.

Books by Kim Lawrence

HARLEQUIN PRESENTS®
2034—ACCIDENTAL BABY

KIM LAWRENCE

Wedding-Night Baby

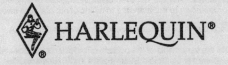

TORONTO • NEW YORK • LONDON
AMSTERDAM • PARIS • SYDNEY • HAMBURG
STOCKHOLM • ATHENS • TOKYO • MILAN • MADRID
PRAGUE • WARSAW • BUDAPEST • AUCKLAND

ISBN 0-373-12053-2

WEDDING-NIGHT BABY

First North American Publication 1999.

Copyright © 1997 by Kim Lawrence.

This edition published by arrangement with Harlequin Books S.A.

Printed in U.S.A.

CHAPTER ONE

GEORGINA TRIED the deep-crowned straw hat once more before discarding it in favour of the cream silk creation which looked for all the world like an oversized mushroom. It did amazingly kind things to her heart-shaped face. She was experimenting with tucking her long chestnut hair into the crown when the doorbell rang. Apprehension shadowed the clear depths of her thickly fringed hazel eyes.

This would be him! With a deep breath that was meant to go some way towards making her appear calm and collected, she went to answer the door of her flat. She opened the door with a flourish, but as her eyes travelled upwards to the face of the man on her threshold her studied smile faltered and died, to be replaced by a frown that drew her dark, well-defined brows into a straight line.

There had to be some mistake! Her heart sank as she took in the teak-skinned, hawkish face; this wasn't what she had been expecting at all! How would this creature conduct himself at a social function? He hardly looked house-trained! And besides, he wasn't even wearing morning dress, after she had specifically stated… She'd never believe any recommendation of Bea's again!

Indignation made her draw herself up to her full, but unimpressive, height. Just for a split second she had had the strangest notion she had seen him before, which was absurd, of course—this wasn't the sort of man a person forgot! Not the sort of man she needed at all. But the odd electrical spasm of recognition that had prickled along her nerve fibres was too definite to ignore totally. Rather than analyse the disconcerting sensation, she found it easier to concentrate on the aggravation his physical appearance might well cause her.

'Miss Campion...?' She noted with some indignation that the tall stranger looked almost as taken aback as she felt. His blue eyes were running over her pink suit with a bemused expression. The narrowing of those eyes was a frown without any other movement of his rock-hard features; this was probably as near to disconcerted as his features went.

Suddenly she wished she'd opted for a longer skirt-length, and whilst she had thought at the time that combining pink with her hair was a statement meant to break down stereotypical colour co-ordination it now seemed a major error. This was foolish, because aside from the fact that all her hair was concealed a man in his line of work who didn't even possess morning dress was no great arbiter of good taste.

'I asked for tails,' she informed him sternly. The blue eyes blinked, but he didn't exactly look stricken by this information. 'Still, it is optional and that suit isn't too bad,' she admitted grudgingly; the fabric and cut made it almost appear a designer creation, though his long-limbed body would probably make most things look better than average. Her eyes travelled the length of his body and she swallowed—a lot better, she conceded grudgingly. Common sense told her that a man who made his living this way couldn't run to designer labels. 'You'd better come in.'

'You *are* Miss Georgina Campion?' He was very tall, she realised as he ducked to avoid a low light-fitting in her tiny hallway. His voice was gravelly, deep and held a vague twang which she couldn't immediately identify; it was slight and she couldn't place it.

She felt flustered and ill at ease as she confirmed her identity. His composure was a stark contrast as he looked around curiously—but then, she reminded herself, for him this was a commonplace situation. No wonder he seemed remarkably at ease. Still, all the better if he was professional, she told herself soothingly.

'Have we met before?' The frown returned to his penetrating eyes and the query had a vaguely accusing note to it.

'I have the sort of face that reminds people of their distant cousins,' she said, realising with a start that her instantaneous reaction had not been unilateral. Unless, of course, this was the man's clumsy attempt at being agreeable. It didn't seem likely; nothing else about him suggested that he was going out of his way to be more than basically polite. 'Under the circumstances you'd better make it Georgina. My family call me Georgie, but I hate it,' she warned him sharply.

'Anyone would,' he observed in a soothing manner. A slight spasm around his mouth seemed to indicate that he found this admission amusing. 'Georgina is a charming name.'

She viewed the gravity in his face with suspicion but only gave a small grunt in reply. 'Come in. I've left your buttonhole in the fridge. If we don't get a move on we'll be late.'

She fetched the white carnation from its resting place and returned to her sitting room to find her escort casually flicking through her books. He glanced up as she entered. With him beside her she was certainly going to be conspicuous, she decided, not sure whether this was desirable or not.

'I suppose, under the circumstances, I'd better know your name,' she said, handing him the flower and pinning on her own corsage of delicate Singapore orchids.

'It's Callum.' Struggling with her corsage, she didn't see the sudden decisive narrowing of his alert eyes. 'Callum…Smith,' he finished smoothly, moving forward as she pricked her finger with the pin. The minor manipulation of the truth didn't cause him any qualms.

Despite the jet lag and the will-reading he'd had to attend Callum suddenly felt less tired. He had already decided that Miss Georgina Campion must be an unusually astute young woman. The size of the personal bequest which his uncle had left instructions for him to deliver personally made that much obvious, but she wasn't what he'd expected at all.

It might be worth his while finding out what it was about her that the old fox, Oliver, had found so appealing—beyond the obvious, he thought with a cynical twist to his lips. He didn't actually begrudge her the money, just the way she'd got it.

So far the trip hadn't gone as smoothly as he'd anticipated. He had hoped to find an heir apparent already installed on his uncle's throne. It had become immediately obvious to him that this wasn't so. He was irritated that he would have to spend more time in London than he had originally intended. He wasn't anxious to become embroiled in business which didn't interest him.

Since he'd got here he'd found the same name cropping up, first of all at the solicitor's and then once again when he'd reached Mallory's. It was highly suspect that she seemed to be the only person privy to essential information. Coming face to face with his uncle's lady-friend had been something of a shock, but he wasn't about to be misled by a pair of wide eyes and an air of innocence.

'Let me,' he offered smoothly, taking the flowers from her fingers. Her youth and innocent appearance must have appealed to an elderly though still robust man. No doubt she knew exactly how to manipulate all her advantages, he thought, distaste filling him as he smiled brilliantly. His interest was piqued—more than piqued, if he was honest.

How his family and friends would stare if they knew he was ready to act on impulse and embark on this bizarre blind date—Callum Stewart, whose behaviour was always governed by cool, clear logic. He justified his actions by telling himself he'd find out more about her if she didn't view him as a danger.

Georgina stuck her bleeding thumb in her mouth and remained stationary whilst he fixed her corsage against the bodice of her jacket. It was the sort of top that was meant to be worn with nothing underneath, and whilst the neckline was respectable the deep V did hint at the cleavage it only just concealed. Georgina wished she knew just what those blue eyes could see with the advantage of height.

'There, all done.' He took a step back, not lingering over his task. The waft of his breath on her cheek was warm and fragrant and the tip of his forefinger as it grazed her neck felt slightly calloused, although his long, shapely fingers were neatly manicured. Georgina was annoyed to find she'd been holding her breath whilst the task was accomplished.

Hiring an escort for the day suddenly seemed a less sensible decision than it had before she'd actually met him. Callum Smith wasn't the sort of man she had wanted at all. Beneath the well-cut suit was a body that looked lethally powerful. He looked quite out of place in the suburban setting—impressive, but not at all domesticated. The strong-boned face was in no way pretty but it was fiercely commanding, with all the confidence and hauteur of a hawk.

She gave herself a mental shake. Hawk indeed! She was being fanciful; the tan was probably nothing more than overexposure to a sunbed, and the impressive build the result of many narcissistic hours in a gym, pumping iron.

He was what she'd got, and he'd have to do for the day. All that stark, unrelenting masculinity was going to be tough to take for an entire day; she preferred a slightly more subdued appeal in her men.

Not that I actually have any, she reminded herself stoically, ignoring the emotional tightening in her throat as she acknowledged her solitary state.

'I don't suppose you have a car. We'll use mine,' she added as he didn't contradict her. 'We should start now; I have to nurse her on the motorway,' she explained, gathering her handbag.

'Where are we going?'

She shot him an exasperated look. 'To my cousin's wedding in Somerset. Doesn't that agency tell you anything?' she grumbled. She was being freshly assailed by doubts about this scheme. Bea had been so convincing and she had scoffed at Georgina's rather prim enquiries as to how respectable these escorts were. Georgina had wanted to make it quite clear at the outset that *all* she wanted was a piece of window-dressing for one day.

'Maybe you should go over the details just in case they've forgotten anything else,' he suggested as he followed her down the steps she shared with the four other tenants of the old Edwardian semi.

'I probably should,' Georgina agreed. The battered Beetle was where she had left it in the shared parking space. About to duck in through the door, she thought better of the operation and took off her hat, laying it carefully on the rear seat. 'It's open,' she told her companion, who was staring, quite rudely, at her hair. It was thick and glossy, a deep shade of russet, her best asset—her only asset, she sometimes thought. It fell, river-straight and glossy, to her waist.

With ill-concealed amusement she watched him attempt to fold his long, lean frame into the passenger seat.

'Doesn't this blasted thing adjust?' he asked as he finally managed to squash himself in. 'No wonder you leave it open; no one in their right mind would steal this death trap.'

'It did adjust once, but it's stuck. You'd better put your seat belt on; I wouldn't want your neck on my conscience. If it's any comfort I have a legitimate MOT.' What was he used to—chauffeur-driven limousines?

'You'll have more than my neck on your conscience if I have to travel far in this thing. Couldn't you get a cab?'

She laughed as she started the engine. 'All the way to Somerset? I'm not made of money. Don't worry,' she added, in case he got the wrong idea. 'I can pay your fee.'

'I'm relieved,' he observed drily. 'I could drive,' he added tensely as she negotiated a bend.

'I wouldn't have thought you could afford to be chauvinistic in your line of work,' she shot back, ruffled at the implied criticism of her driving. Then, in case she'd wounded his feelings, she added, 'Not that there's anything wrong with your line of work.'

Work of any sort was hard enough to come by these days. Perhaps the man had family responsibilities, or he was out of work. Casting a sidelong glance at his profile, she had to admit he didn't look like someone harassed by domestic detail. She was anxious in case she'd sounded prudish and judgemental.

'Have you used the agency often?' he enquired casually.

'Never before, but my friend Bea has several times. Lots of women are too busy to have a relationship and certain social occasions can be uncomfortable without a male escort.' She darted a glare at her companion, daring him to contradict her, uncomfortably aware that she was trying to convince herself as much as him.

The blue eyes were fixed on her profile and she swiftly

averted her gaze to the road, finding the intensity of the startling blue glare disorientating.

'I'm sure you're right, but I doubt if that state of affairs would continue for long... You're a very attractive lady.'

Georgina gritted her teeth. 'I'm sure you have a very nice line in insincere compliments,' she hissed, 'but I'd like to make it quite clear that I require an attentive, presentable escort, nothing more.'

'Just an observation.' He'd seen more attractive women, known truly beautiful women, experienced instant attraction and sometimes done something about it, but never before had he experienced such an immediate and urgent desire to touch, to claim a woman in a profoundly primal way.

This visceral reaction had been triggered by the briefest touching of eyes. The muscles in his belly still contracted as he recalled the blind bondage of that fleeting instant before his brain had started to function with its usual clarity. Callum frowned; he had every intention of keeping his hormones in check.

Georgina made a disgruntled sound of disbelief in her throat. She'd have to make it quite clear from the outset that she was not some pathetic female who had to hire a man to flatter her. He was window-dressing and he'd better remember it, she thought grimly.

'What's your cousin's name? I really should have a little background information, to make things look realistic. I have my reputation to think of,' he observed reasonably, entering into the spirit of the thing.

'Harriet. She's marrying a solicitor, Alex Taylor, who, as you'll no doubt hear, dumped me about eighteen months ago.' Chin high, she crunched her gears noisily at a junction. 'Hence the need for an attentive escort. You, Mr Smith, are a face-saving device,' she told him, making a clean breast of the matter. In one way it was a relief to have someone she didn't have to keep up appearances with; it didn't matter what Callum Smith thought of her.

'You couldn't take all the sympathetic glances and whispers?' He was silently congratulating himself on his decision to follow his instincts where this woman was concerned. She didn't feel obliged to employ any artifice with him; he was only the hired help. If she knew who he was he would be seeing quite a different picture; of that he was sure.

'Precisely,' she replied, relieved he was quick on the uptake. 'I suppose you've been in similar situations before.'

'Not precisely like this,' he observed truthfully. 'But I'm quite resourceful,' he added with almost languid confidence as she cast him a look of alarm.

'I hope so,' she said fervently.

'Couldn't you have got a friend to help you out today?'

'Meaning I don't have any friends or I wouldn't have resorted to hiring you?'

'Now there's an interesting thought.'

Georgina flicked him a brief, fulminating glare before gritting her teeth. 'I come from a small village where the fact that my cousin is marrying provides hours of entertainment. I don't want to expose a friend to that sort of curiosity. I need someone who can disappear without trace. Someone presentable, but—'

'Forgettable?'

She grudgingly nodded her agreement. 'You'll stick out like a sore thumb,' she complained, her mobile mouth pursing as she considered her ill luck.

'Why's that?' he enquired, evincing interest.

'We've had about two days' insipid sun so far this summer; you look too tanned,' she said critically. The fact was that he was far too arresting to fade into the background, but she wasn't about to feed his ego; she felt sure he knew perfectly well what she meant. Under normal circumstances a man like him wouldn't be seen with a girl as ordinary as her. 'Don't you know sunbeds are bad for the skin? Skin cancer!' she elaborated darkly.

'I'm touched by your concern but I've been working overseas, outdoors.'

'Manual work?' That would explain the splendid physique.

'Don't worry, it's not catching.'

The disdain in his voice made her flush angrily. 'I don't give a damn if you're an itinerant labourer or a brain surgeon so long as you don't blow this for me. There's nothing wrong with manual work.'

'I feel better already.'

'I'm glad one of us does,' she said grimly. She'd had enough of the objectionable Callum Smith and the day had hardly begun!

CHAPTER TWO

THE VILLAGE CHURCH was the same one in which she had imagined herself walking down the aisle with Alex, and now she'd have to smilingly watch her cousin make that journey she'd so longed for. I don't care any more, she told herself firmly as the constricting waves of emotion rose to suffocate her. She had no intention of wallowing in self-pity even though the temptation was strong.

She started as Callum held the door open for her; she hadn't noticed him get out of the car.

'Thank you, Mr Smith,' she said, ignoring his outstretched hand.

'I think you'd better make that Callum, in the interests of authenticity,' he observed drily. 'Don't forget the hat.' Slightly narrowed eyes had taken in at a glance all the tiny details of stress in the face of the girl beside him. She was hiding it well, but the tautness about her mouth and the rigidity of her usually mobile features gave away the inner turmoil. He found his eyes strangely reluctant to leave her slightly parted pink lips.

Flustered and mildly resentful because he appeared to be taking charge, Georgina grabbed the silky mushroom and crammed it on her head, tucking strands of her hair into the crown. 'How's that?'

'You missed a bit.' He took hold of a strand that had slithered down her neck and slid it under the fabric rim, recalling as he did so that he'd heard her referred to as 'Miss Efficiency' in scornful tones very recently. At the moment she looked very young and quite appalling vulnerable. Was that how she'd got to the old fox? he wondered cynically.

His fingers were very long, Georgina noticed as she gave a small, delicate shiver. The slight touch of faintly calloused fingertips against her throat was distracting, though not exactly unpleasant, she conceded. In fact, it was quite nice to be distracted from the ordeal ahead. 'Charming. I'm sure the groom will be consumed with regret,' he said, his lips twisting cynically.

'I really couldn't give a damn,' she said haughtily. The implied criticism made her bristle defensively.

'What a little trouper.' The mockery was even more apparent this time, but before she had time to put him firmly in his place she found that one of his arms had snaked around her waist, his dark, tanned face was close to her own, and he was laughing huskily as though she'd just said something wildly witty.

'What the...?'

'Wedding guests at ten o'clock, closing fast,' he hissed close to her ear. For good measure he nibbled said orifice. For some reason her eyes closed and a shiver went right down to her toes.

Blinking, she stared into the intense blue eyes. Deep tramlines radiated from the corners, and his lashes, whilst dark and thick, were straight. They weren't just arresting eyes; they gave the impression of intelligence and humour, and a certain implacability shone clearly in the azure depths. He wasn't just a physically overpowering person; intellectually, even on the briefest of acquaintances, he gave the impression of being a force to be reckoned with.

Escort could not have been the first choice of career for him. What personal circumstances had reduced him...? It's none of my business, she told herself, closing this line of speculation as a familiar voice broke her trance.

'Georgie, is that you, darling? I didn't recognise you. Did you, George? We were just talking about you...so brave. Still, better to find out these things early on.'

Georgina bit her lip as she nodded placidly at this trite observation. 'Aunt Helen, Uncle George,' she said quietly. The arm around her waist was suddenly very welcome. 'This is Callum,' she said triumphantly, much with the manner of a magician pulling a rabbit out of a hat. But there the similarity ended. If Callum was to be likened to anything in the animal kingdom he was much more like a large, sleek, predatory cat.

Callum took the scrutiny of her relations in his stride. In fact, he seemed to have adopted a certain air of authority that made them look away first.

'I meet some of Georgina's relations at last,' he said, enveloping her uncle's hand in a grip that made the older man wince slightly. The kiss he planted on her aunt's cheek made her blush and look as flustered as any teenager. 'Charming church,' he observed, glancing at the square stone building. 'Norman, isn't it?' He took Georgina's hand and intertwined his fingers with her own. 'Am I speaking to the parents of the blushing bride?'

'Indeed you are,' Georgina agreed, bringing forth her very best not-a-care-in-the-world smile.

Blushing bride! Her dear cousin was far too hard-baked ever to blush. Harriet had awaited her opportunity and stalked Alex with all the cunning and guile of a jungle animal. Georgina had always known her cousin coveted her boyfriend. It was the fact that her unassailable belief that Alex would never even look at another woman had been proved false that made her inwardly cringe. Had she ever been that naïve? When it came to the crunch he'd done a lot more than look!

But it's useless to go over old ground, she told herself as she felt the familiar sensation of impotent fury rise.

With my family history I should have known better. Well, I *do* know better now, she thought, her chin lifting.

Callum held the lych-gate to the churchyard open and waited for the older couple to pass through. 'Smile,' he hissed as they followed, still hand in hand. 'You look like you're on your way to the scaffold,' he added.

Georgina's eyes glittered with wrath and she struggled to withdraw her fingers. 'I thought you were here to butter me up?' she breathed angrily. This man had forgotten his passive role very thoroughly. He had no right to make personal comments.

He stopped in his tracks and jerked her around to face him. 'I didn't think you liked insincere compliments?'

'I'm not too keen on insults either.'

'I have my professional pride to consider,' he told her gravely. 'I would appreciate a little co-operation. Unless you relish the role of early Christian martyr?'

This question made her bite her lip. He was right, of course. She had to act a part in order to salvage her battered pride. '*I'm* not a professional,' she reminded him. 'And I find it strange...your being a total stranger.'

'Live your part, Georgina; we're a hot item,' he contradicted her. His lips brushed hers, gently, but with a confident familiarity. 'I thought all girls could fake it?' His lips quirked in a deeply cynical smile.

'I'm sure the girls you know can,' she responded acidly. 'Do you think you could limit that sort of authenticity to the basic minimum?' she added, drawing away, her colour noticeably heightened. She summoned a distracted but brilliant smile for the usher, a boy she'd known since school.

'Georgie?' he said, a note of doubt in his voice. He flushed as she gave him a quizzical look, and continued hurriedly, 'Bride or groom? Silly question; you'd hardly be with the groom, would you?' The expression of ludicrous dismay that spread over his face made Georgina feel almost sympathetic.

'We'll find our own way, thank you, Jim,' she said crisply, sweeping past him. 'That's my mother,' she said to the man beside her in a hushed undertone as they entered the dim, ecclesiastical atmosphere of the old building. She nodded in the general direction of one of the front pews.

'Pink hat?' Callum had bent his head to catch her hissed words.

Georgina nodded. 'We'll clash marvellously; she'll be furious,' she observed fatalistically. 'I should have known; Mother's a pink sort of person.' She led him self-consciously to the front of the church.

'Georgie, what possessed you to wear pink with your hair?' Lydia Campion was a beautiful woman whose stern features had been softened by the years. As always she looked stunningly elegant. Georgina knew she could never achieve that degree of polish—the lie of the silk scarf, the tilt of the chin. To Lydia it was as simple as breathing; to her it took hours of painstaking consideration, and even then she was only halfway there.

Georgina shot her companion a tiny I-told-you-so look, before sitting down on the pew.

'Mrs Campion, I have to take full responsibility for the outfit. Georgina was humouring me.'

The look of shock on her mother's face as Callum, all eighteen-carat charm and charisma, bent forward across her and extended his hand made Georgina, despite the gravity of her situation, want to giggle. This was not the type of man her mother or anyone else expected good old Georgie to be with. For the first time since she'd seen Callum Smith she felt that her decision to employ a little face-saving artifice had been justified. Might as well utilise his slightly dangerous air for what it was worth. She was the only one to know how fake the glamour was.

'He's colour-blind,' Georgina added with a faint quiver in her voice.

This frivolous comment earned her a swift frown from her parents. 'Who is this, Georgina? Where are your manners?'

'This is Callum Sm—'

'Delighted to meet you, Mrs Campion.'

'Do call me Lydia. You're a friend of Georgie's? She is so secretive.'

'A little more than that, eh, sweetheart?' Callum's impossibly deep blue gaze was fixed on her face with teasing affection. The warm, rich, bitter-chocolate tones just hinted at unspoken intimacies. He was so incredibly convincing that she found herself blushing deeply.

At that moment a figure on the periphery of her vision rose from the row of pews just opposite her. Her head turned as if pulled by invisible strings and her stomach muscles clenched painfully.

The first time she'd seen him she'd been blind to everything else, but now she was uncomfortably conscious of the man beside her. Disturbingly she wanted to turn her head and look at him. The memory of the fleeting sensation she'd experienced when she'd first seen him washed over her. Had Alex *ever* made her feel like that? What a ridiculous time to admit how physically attractive she found her escort, she told herself crossly.

Alex was an extremely good-looking young man, tallish, athletic. His features were regular, his expression sincere and forthright. The teeth were standard toothpaste-advert stuff and his naturally blond hair was highlighted with exquisite restraint.

The loss and bitterness she felt were suddenly physical. When Alex's eyes passed over her without any sign of recognition she didn't know whether to be glad or devastated. The city gloss she'd worked hard to achieve obviously worked. Pity she was still the same girl underneath the expensive clothes and make-up.

The large hand that suddenly clasped her jaw woke her from the short, intense abstraction. As her head turned life flowed back into her body, and it hurt, like icy fingers when the circulation in them began to move once more. 'I take exception when a woman with me looks at another man like a drooling idiot.' Low, conversational, his words made her blink. His face had come in close, the whole incident having the appearance of intimacy.

'How dare you?' she spat. The arrogance of the man was breathtaking. 'So long as you're paid, it's no concern of yours what I do. Don't get carried away with your role,' she advised tartly. She felt humiliated at being caught out in the sort of behaviour she'd sworn to herself she'd not indulge in. Her anger, perfectly logically, was aimed at the only person who'd noticed her momentary weakness and who had had the tasteless effrontery to mention the fact.

'It's a waste of time to spend money on a love-struck swain if you behave with the discretion of an adolescent. Why should I waste my time and effort to act the lover if you aren't going to co-operate?'

She was instantly stung by the insinuation that to act the lover required a vast amount of effort. 'Because you're being paid to do so,' she hissed venomously. 'So save the temperament. What are you anyway—an out-of-work actor? If you must know, you aren't at *all* what I wanted. I require an escort, not a soul mate, so stop working so hard. Unless you're an excellent liar you'll end up making fools of us both. My mother's interrogation techniques are honed to perfection,' she told him drily, aware of the sharp eyes watching their every move.

He gave a snort. 'If that—' he jerked his head in the

direction of the groom '—is your taste, I find it easy to
believe I'm not what the doctor ordered. Take a dummy
from the average shop window and you could have a fac-
simile of your perfect mate.' The curl of his lip was openly
derisory.

Her bosom swelled with outrage. 'How dare you?' The
long-entrenched habit of thinking Alex encapsulated masculine perfection made her eyes flash.

'Without any great effort,' he murmured with casual,
almost bored provocation. 'You do keep saying that, or
hadn't you noticed? Repetition is a sign of a limited intellect, so I've heard.'

'Do they employ many intellectual giants at the escort
agency?' she was pushed into responding sarcastically.

'One for every snobbish client.'

Absurdly she felt suddenly apprehensive; there was
something about the softness in his voice and the contrast-
ing hardness in his deceptively guileless eyes Mentally
she shook herself for having such fanciful thoughts. After
today she would never have to see this man again; he had
no influence upon her life. Still, he did have a point she
would have to pull herself together if she was going to
convince anyone she was totally heart-whole and leading
a completely satisfying life.

Which, of course, she was. She had a stimulating career
as a personal assistant in an advertising agency. A frown
furrowed her wide, smooth brow as she thought of the man
who had, up until recently, been her boss. Oliver Mallory,
the infamous hand that had guided the well-known firm to
its present place as one of the top six advertising agencies
in the country. She had been his protégée and he had been
her friend. Oliver had built the agency up from nothing
and now he was gone. Though this left her own position
uncertain, it was genuine sadness at the loss of the dear
old reprobate that made her sigh.

She had everything she had wanted—a career, a flat of her own, independence, good friends, freedom—but without a man at her side she knew that her friends and relations would see only a jilted woman. The widely held conviction that a woman needed a man for fulfilment was one she personally detested. She had seen her own mother go through a series of temporary affairs of the heart, each one leaving her a little more desperate and lonely than the last. Her own recent experience of loss had made her determined never to repeat it.

'Do you mind taking your hands off me?' she said, raising her lowered eyes to the face of the man who was, given the time and place, in socially unacceptable proximity to her.

The hand that had captured her attention still lay along the line of her jaw; the tips of his fingers were burrowed into her hairline. His bent head was level with her own, close enough for her to be able to admire the texture of his bronzed skin, smell the masculine fragrance that drifted from him.

One of his fingers worked its way around a stray lock of hair that had escaped the confines of her wildly expensive headgear. The expression in his heavy-lidded, shadowed eyes as they watched the temporary corkscrew effect of his casual labour was absurdly riveting. Also the hard thigh pressed against her own on the wooden seat was distracting—unpleasantly so, she told herself, frowning as a pack of butterflies ran riot in the pit of her stomach.

The familiar strains of the Bridal March issued forth from the organ and, heart thudding, she pulled free, giving her escort a cold, dismissive look, as much to convince herself that he had nothing to do with the adrenaline surge that sent her heart against her ribcage as anything else. At a time like this she couldn't possibly spare a second thought for anything but the main event.

The bride was tiresomely lovely, her responses clear and resonant. It was the groom who sounded less than his usual confident self. Georgina waited for the humiliation of the occasion to hit her, but with a sense of anticlimax she realised that she was able to view the whole ceremony with detachment. It was like watching a scene of a play she felt totally uninvolved.

Outside the sun did its duty and the guests huddled together whilst photographs were taken. Her lips curled in a cynical smile, Georgina watched her mother speaking with some animation to a distinguished-looking man she didn't recognise. She kept her chin high and replied cheerfully to greetings from familiar faces, who looked at the tall figure at her side with varying degrees of curiosity, tinged in some cases, she was amused to see, with envy. Well, it was infinitely preferable to pity, she told herself.

'Why did he ditch you?'

'That's an extremely insensitive question,' she observed, stiffening. Her paid company was watching the proceedings with an air of impatient boredom.

'I've never been one to indulge maudlin self-pity.'

'Or one to keep your opinions to yourself, it would seem.'

'Just displaying a friendly interest.'

'Just fishing for the salacious details, more like.'

The thick dark brows shot towards his hairline. 'Salacious? I was just trying to make conversation, but now I'm really interested.' The gleam of humour in his eyes was faintly malicious.

'Actually, it was all very civilised. I went to London to do a business-studies course. We weren't engaged or anything,' she said with a detached smile, skimming sketchily over an emotional blow that had devastated her.

'Everyone, including you, expected marriage,' he observed shrewdly.

It was peculiar, but his neutral cynicism was much easier to cope with than the understanding sympathy that had been doled out to her at the time. 'There was an understanding,' she agreed, switching her weight from one foot to the other and checking who was within hearing distance. It would never do to have this conversation overheard.

She'd agreed that a ring was an extravagance when she and Alex were saving so assiduously. Strange how Harriet had managed to get a serious diamond on her finger in record time, she thought cynically. That was probably why Alex had exchanged his racy coupé for a more sedate saloon. Harriet was worth the sacrifice, it would seem.

'Did you put up much of a fight? Or had you already got someone more interesting lined up? That can't have been difficult,' Callum said, his mind returning to this girl's relationship with his uncle. Her rather full lips had drooped slightly. For someone who gave off such an air of wholesome sexiness her mouth was altogether more...sensual. A more accurate indication of her character? he wondered. Had her unorthodox manner of promotion been the bone of contention between lovers?

'No man is worth fighting for,' she replied, her tone ringing with grim conviction.

Callum caught her arm and swung her out of the path of a gaggle of small pages and bridesmaids. 'Isn't that a rather sweeping statement?'

'I prefer comprehensive and accurate.' The arm casually draped around her waist showed no inclination to shift. Rather than make herself conspicuous, she let it stay there. She hoped her attitude showed him how totally oblivious to the near proximity she was.

'After getting your fingers burnt once?' he said incredulously. 'Or am I to infer you have a more chequered past than that?'

His cynical, knowing expression made her long to throttle him. 'I know you're bored, but I'm not about to enliven your afternoon with any juicy stories. My mother will track you down any moment and extract your vital juices,' she said darkly and with some relish. Some people deserved her mother.

It was irritating to have to raise her chin to look into his face. Alex was just the perfect height—especially when he'd kissed her, she recalled wistfully. What would it be like to be kissed by this man? Dry-mouthed, she allowed the thought to crystallise with clarity in her head. Swallowing with difficulty, she killed this frivolous piece of speculation and lowered her eyes, which might be less obedient than her brain.

'She seems occupied at present,' Callum observed, glancing towards the spot where Lydia stood with the middle-aged guest.

'Predictably so.' Her mother was laughing—a low, husky sound that grated on Georgina's frayed nerves.

'Do I detect criticism from the daughter? Ought you not to have grown out of the desire to view your parent as a sexless entity? I take it your father is no longer around?'

She wriggled her hips decisively and his hands intuitively fell away from her waist. Where did he get off analysing and criticising her?

'For your information my father has never been around—at least, not since I was born. He walked out on her, unable to take the strain of domesticity,' she drawled sarcastically. 'But Mother never gives up. Her life is not complete without a man on her arm and in her bed. In a place like this the fact doesn't pass without comment. But they all slip away eventually. Like mother, like daughter— we obviously can't hold our men—' Breathing hard, she stopped abruptly and bit hard on her trembling lip, appalled at what she'd just said to a total stranger.

The unvarnished distress emanating from her was unsettling to Callum. He quashed any chivalrous instincts. He wasn't about to let sentiment interfere with his original reason for seeking out Miss Campion. 'Are you going to faint?' He tried to sound unalarmed at the prospect but the violent fluctuation of her colour made him suspect the worst.

The grin was sudden and surprising, full of self-mockery and quite unintentionally charming. 'Throw up, more likely,' she said frankly. 'But don't worry; it's passed. I'd be grateful if you'd forget what I just said.'

He met the direct, almost green stare squarely. 'Your hang-ups are your business, lady,' he drawled, his accent slightly more pronounced than usual. He touched his forehead as if saluting. The casual elegant gesture had none of the military about it.

Her lips tightened. 'How do you manage to make everything you say sound like a judgement? Does it ever occur to you you're in the wrong line of work? A charming, relaxing companion was what I was promised... Instead I got the Grand Inquisitor.'

'If you're not satisfied you can always complain. I'll probably lose my job.' The sigh was stoical. 'But don't let that deter you; we live in a consumer society. There's no place for sentiment.'

She had to grin; he did 'meek' rather well. 'Just try and look pretty and don't say too much,' she advised.

'Sexist,' he mumbled as they were ushered into a photo line-up.

The top table was not where she'd hoped to find herself placed. She scented Cousin Harriet's hand in this arrangement; she always had been less than generous in victory. A great believer in salt rubbed firmly in the wound, our dear Harriet. Still, if she sat far enough back in her seat the depth of Callum's impressive torso gave her some defence from the sight of the happy couple. The voices were not so easy to block out.

She'd wasted her breath telling Callum to keep his mouth in a strait-jacket. He'd been in earnest conversation with her uncle George for the past ten minutes. She couldn't catch everything they were saying, but financial terms kept drifting in her direction. He might be a good con artist but her uncle made a very successful living as a financial advisor and it was only a matter of time before he discovered that Callum didn't know what he was talking about.

She picked worriedly at her fish and drank her wine faster than was advisable on an empty stomach. One ear on an elderly relative on her left, she tried to hear what Callum was saying in his rather deep voice, waiting for her uncle's respectful expression to turn to scorn.

Callum intercepted her sidelong glance and winked, his expression not changing as he continued to expand on his subject.

Angrily she accepted the wine waiter's solicitous offer of a refill and swigged it back with scant regard for an expensive vintage. He'd laugh on the other side of his face when she spoke to the agency, she thought militantly. It might be a joke to him... A lump of self-pity rose in her throat as Harriet's laughter made her teeth clench.

'Callum, dar-r-rling,' she purred. Her nails made inroads into the hand she affectionately covered on the damask tablecloth. 'You really mustn't talk business. You promised,' she added, her eyes flashing warnings. If it hurt he managed to disguise the fact remarkably well.

With a flash of white teeth he picked up her claw-like hand and pressed it, open-palmed, to his lips. The gesture was more erotic than courtly.

Her eyes were caught in the bold, mocking glare of his regard. The explosion of heat that flooded across her skin must have been evident to him; it was a response that appalled and disgusted her, a physical thing over which she had no control. The confusion of churning sensations in her belly was profoundly basic and instinctual and she was ashamed of being susceptible to the brazen sexuality of this man. The wine obviously had a good deal to do with this uninhibited response.

'Are you feeling neglected, angel?' The dark brows lifted, but she could see the acknowledgement in his eyes of her helpless, angry response. 'That will never do,' he murmured huskily, and he let his lips move once more over her hand.

If she could have, she'd have climbed out of her skin. Her nerve-endings were on fire, screaming. Dry-mouthed, she shifted in her seat fretfully.

Uncle George regarded them indulgently. 'My fault, Georgie, dear. You've got a sound man there,' he said approvingly.

This unexpected recommendation made Georgina's fuming silence lengthen. Her uncle was not the sort of man who threw compliments around lightly. 'You always were a sterling judge of character, Uncle George,' she said drily. The man she loved was barely feet from her and here she was, suffering contemptible, primitive responses to a stranger. It was morally indefensible; worse still, she hadn't had the sense to hide it.

'Will you behave?' she said in a furious undertone as she pulled her hand free.

'In what particular way did you have in mind?' he enquired with interest. He winced as girlish laughter rang out once more. 'You know, I think you should pity that stuffed shirt of yours. He'll have to live with that laugh for the rest of his natural. Always supposing things last that long.'

'I wish them all the best,' she observed primly.

'Lying little hypocrite,' he said conversationally. He

swirled the liquid in his glass around but didn't lift it to his lips. 'Like all females you're a vindictive little beast who can't wait to see the man grovel at your feet.'

'I can well believe the females in *your* life feel that way,' she responded tartly. She had rehearsed the tender scene of Alex turning up begging her forgiveness once too often to look him directly in the eye. 'I don't find the role of plucky little victim to my taste; that's the *only* reason you're here. I have no wish to make Alex jealous, which, considering what I got for my money, is just as well.'

The deep blue eyes narrowed to slits and his lips twisted with scornful amusement. 'You're comparing me unfavourably to that?' he said with a scornful lift of his shoulders and a flickering glance in Alex's direction.

'You really do think a lot of yourself, don't you?'

'My self-esteem was fairly healthy last time I looked,' he agreed.

'If I had a large pin I'd like to deflate it,' she murmured longingly. 'Only I'd call it ego.'

'Your nose was never constructed to be looked down, sweetheart.'

'I'm well aware of my physical deficiencies, thank you!' she replied tartly. With a mother who was an acknowledged beauty she couldn't help but be. Her nose was unremarkable, her mouth too big. She gave a small sigh. People who were obsessed with their appearance often neglected their personality, or so she often found—if they had any at all. She wasn't about to fall into that trap.

'I wouldn't say it's a deficiency. I'd call it kind of cute.' The blue eyes which examined the sudden rush of colour that stained her cheeks looked remarkably guileless. 'Say, I know today's a real traumatic experience for you, so why don't we forget the rotten mongrel who humiliated you and relax? The food's good, the wine could be better but it's plentiful, and I won't blow your cover. Lighten up, eat, drink and dance a little. Enjoy the charming company you've paid for.'

'Charming?' She couldn't help smiling.

'I have a reputation to uphold,' he told her solemnly. 'Is it a deal?'

The smile bordered on the irresistible, so recklessly she raised her glass and found herself agreeing.

CHAPTER THREE

'GEORGIE, he's absolutely gorgeous, darling. Where did you find him?'

'Yellow Pages, Alice,' she told her drooling school-friend with a grin. Callum was dancing with the bride, displaying remarkable grace and co-ordination for such a large man.

'You never used to be so enigmatic,' her friend grumbled, her eyes on Callum's progress across the floor. 'You even look different.' Her eyes moved critically over her old friend's slender figure.

Georgina hardly heard. The man might be abominably conceited, she reflected, her eyes too on the tall figure, but he did have some reason. Controlled power, languid grace and an ability to make everyone present hang on his every word were all attributes that she privately thought could be put to better use in some other capacity than that of hired escort. He had something indefinable but potent; she had given up trying to classify him into any category she had ever come across.

He still remained something of an enigma. Although he had, true to his word, been charming and amusing over the remainder of the meal, he had managed to learn quite a lot about her life, her work and friends whilst unobtrusively redirecting any questions about himself. Why the mystery? she wondered.

He looked up suddenly, his dark features turning intuitively in her direction. Rather than avert her gaze and look elsewhere, she kept her eyes level and her chin square. There was enquiry, a challenge in his bold stare, transmuted as he held her eyes to stark and unadulterated desire.

No man had ever, as far as she could recall, looked at her so brazenly before. The message in his stare was a blatant admission of desire. She had certainly never experienced this flash fire of wildly conflicting sensations. She stood stock-still, caught in the current that passed between them. She recognised that she was a victim of her own primitive cravings, but felt powerless to resist.

With a soft word Callum extricated himself from his partner, who showed an inclination to pout, and moved purposefully across the room.

'This is Alice,' Georgina said nervously as he reached her side.

'Hello, Alice. I haven't danced with Georgina yet. You don't mind if I steal her away, do you?' His eyes only left her face for a second. She was drawn onto the dance floor without even realising she'd relinquished her role as wallflower. 'This day is not turning out at all as I'd expected, Miss Campion.'

'It isn't?' she said thickly. The numbness that had hit her seconds before was slipping away to be replaced by a swamping awareness of her body and its reactions and this man, this stranger who held her, his body. She'd drunk too much. She'd been building up to this day for weeks; it was the stress, the entire cocktail of emotional havoc that was responsible for the sexual awareness that had sprung to life.

'You were described to me as very efficient. I wasn't expecting hair like glossy autumn leaves, soft, buttermilk skin and sultry lips like ripe strawberries.'

She swallowed, frighteningly aware of how much a captive she was of the deep, resonant voice and the glittering eyes. Excitement and a totally alien exhilaration were swirling in her veins. Common sense, with which she knew she was amply endowed, told her that her bruised ego was lapping up this attention because of its traumatised state. But it was difficult to reconcile common sense with the feverish clamour of her blood. She was aware of trembling—a fact he too couldn't have failed to notice.

'Very poetic,' she replied, injecting scorn into her voice and pulling her eyes from the magnetic tug of his gaze. 'This really wasn't in the job description, you know.' She swallowed. How wrong had she been when she'd thought this man was ill-equipped to act as an escort! She'd almost disastrously forgotten that that was what he was. It was the height of stupidity to fall for a look of desire. Do I need to be wanted that much? she thought bitterly. It must be genetic!

'And I'm certain you made that quite clear at the outset.' His voice held a degree of almost amused affection which made her glance up.

'Perhaps that's why the agency described me as efficient.'

'The agency...?' he murmured sharply. 'Oh, yes, the agency. I never mix business with pleasure.' Perhaps this occasion called for a little flexibility, he told himself.

'I'm pleased to hear it,' she said uncertainly. God, how could she be such a fool as to fall for a slick chat-up line and blue eyes? This was superficial attraction, basic. She wished hard that she hadn't addled her senses with all the free wine.

'I'd be more than happy to be your escort on an unpaid basis.'

She was almost sure he was teasing her and the mockery helped her fight the spell that the music, the atmosphere...and Callum were weaving. 'I'm flattered, but you're not the sort of man I'd go out with.'

Callum neatly avoided a collision with a couple who

were both much the worse for the champagne. 'I was thinking more along the lines of staying in,' he admitted with a devilish gleam in his eyes.

The breathless sensation could not be solely attributed to the neat manoeuvre that had swung her around one hundred and eighty degrees. 'I hardly think we're compatible.' She couldn't recall ever being propositioned before so the correct response was difficult to gauge. She was *almost* sure he was joking and it would make her appear ridiculous if she made too much of the incident.

'Strange. I've been getting quite different messages,' he murmured. One hand slid down her hair, letting the heavy, silky strands slide through his fingers. 'Could it be you're afflicted with the great British disease of being unwilling to mingle outside your own class? Would I be a social embarrassment for an upwardly mobile career woman?' Mild but damning contempt liberally coated his words.

'Are you insinuating I'm a snob?' she replied, registering that his scornful words identified him as probably not being British. 'I take it from your smug, egalitarian tone that you don't hail from these shores?'

The slight friction of his hand against the nape of her neck was sending flurries of warmth tingling through her body. His other hand had pulled her body close enough against his own for her to be aware of how taut and muscular his spare frame was. The effort to keep her head from flopping forward against the invitation of his solidly muscled chest made tiny beads of perspiration break out along her upper lip.

'Are you trying to tell me that if I was an eminently respectable professional like your stuffed dummy you'd still be fighting against this attraction?' His eyes gleamed with disdain.

To compare this temporary insanity with what she had felt for Alex might have made her smile under less stressful circumstances. She might have worshipped Alex un-critically and, in retrospect, pathetically, but she had never felt anything nearly so insidiously primitive in his arms. Sometimes she thought her self-restraint had had a lot to do with his seeking comfort elsewhere.

'I've given up on emotional complications in my life.' She wished she sounded as confident about this as she had hoped she would.

'This is more *instinctive* than emotional, don't you think?' he mused, a lick of grim humour in his voice.

When she looked up there was something far more fierce than humour in his eyes—hunger. Her eyes moved of their own volition to his mouth, and the sensuous curl of his lips made her throat close over. The hot, liquid sensation in her belly expanded to flood her already unsteady limbs. The fantasy that passed before her eyes was full of texture and taste. In fact, all her senses seemed to be involved in the concept of this simple, imaginary kiss.

'There speaks the male of the species,' she retorted, her voice all the more angry because of the diversions her mind was taking. 'A physical experience without emotions is an unrewarding one for a woman.'

'I thought you'd given up on emotions?' he said with a quirk of one eyebrow. 'Does this mean you've taken a vow of chastity?'

'Is that so outrageous?'

'I think for some people celibacy might be a possible solution. People with a genuinely asexual personality, that is—those who pretend things they are incapable of feeling just to conform. It's not the answer for someone as sensual as you. Repressing your true nature is no answer.'

'And you'd know all about my personality!' she snapped scornfully.

'I think you're the sort of woman who is afraid to stand up for what she believes in. You're big on independence and self-sufficiency, but when an opportunity to display the fact is offered you, what do you do? Rush off to hire a body to wear a suit so you blend in prettily. It takes guts to stand out, Georgina,' he drawled. 'It seems to me you like to take the safe option.'

His words had homed in on the disquiet she had felt about the entire face-saving exercise. Damn him! she thought, raising her turbulent eyes to his impassive face. 'I take it I'm meant to be forced to display that I'm full of radical action by sleeping with you—not the safe option.'

He appeared unfazed by her hot accusation. 'You have been thinking about it, then,' he said with a small, disturbing smile playing about the corners of his lips.

Her vehement denial died as she met the cynical knowledge in his eyes. She acknowledged she'd just been manoeuvred into a corner by something of an expert. The music had stopped and they stayed stationary in the middle of the floor. Her attention was so concentrated on her partner than she didn't hear Alex the first time he spoke.

'Can I have the next dance, Georgie?'

She spun around, eyes wide, her cheeks still flushed from the stimulation of her fencing with Callum.

'Go ahead, sweetheart,' Callum urged, his hand comfortably patting her behind encouragingly. He regarded the slightly younger man in an almost indulgent manner that visibly grated on Alex. 'The least I can do, as indirectly you're responsible for my meeting Georgina. Incidentally, she hates being called Georgie; didn't she ever tell you?' The music started up and he slipped away, his long strides taking him swiftly out of sight into the crowd.

'Shall we?'

Georgina pulled herself together with a tense smile. She'd been staring after Callum like a hypnotised idiot; embarrassment at this bizarre behaviour brought a fresh rush of colour to her skin. She thought wistfully of the bland partner she'd imagined.

'You look well, Georgie…Georgina,' Alex stumbled awkwardly. 'I hardly recognised you.'

'Should I be flattered? But it's still the same old me, Alex.' Or was she? she wondered, still in daze. The nights of bitterness and heartache, the sense of betrayal and the deep sense of inadequacy she'd fought against with all her will seemed oddly distant as she faced the object of all those thwarted desires.

'You seem different.'

She glanced at him curiously, surprised that she could be objective. He sounded faintly piqued at the transformation, which consisted mostly of a sophisticated outfit and an air of self-confidence that was three parts artifice.

Had Alex ever looked beyond the surface? she wondered. She'd been very young when she'd met him and malleable in many ways. That had suited Alex. The only contention that had ever arisen between them had occurred when she had insisted she wanted more careerwise than a receptionist's job. When she'd insisted on going on her business-studies course, commuting home at weekends, he'd been stiffly disapproving.

'Everyone grows up, Alex,' she observed now, with a wistfulness partly reserved for her lost naïvety. Everyone had known about Alex and Harriet for weeks before she had caught on. The constriction in her throat swelled.

'I treated you pretty badly.'

'Yes,' she agreed, noticing he was the first one to look away. She'd wanted to make him wonder whether he'd made the right decision and, if she read the signs correctly, that was exactly what he was doing. Strange how little pleasure it afforded her. 'Lovely wedding.'

'I wanted something simple.'

'Harriet didn't,' she observed with a faint smile. What Harriet wants, Harriet gets, including my man!

He shrugged awkwardly and she worked hard not to tangle her feet with his. Dancing with Callum had been as easy as breathing—a strange combination of instinct and rhythm. The contrast made her frown.

'Emotional hothouses, weddings,' she said lightly.

'I miss you. I didn't realise how much…'

The words she'd longed to hear filled her with a sudden deep panic. 'I don't think you should be saying this, Alex.' He'd manoeuvred them into a quiet alcove and the drop in volume meant that her voice sounded loud.

'Neither do I.'

Startled, she spun around to see Callum watching them, leaning with negligent ease against a fake Doric pillar.

'I was just…' Alex blustered, letting go of Georgina and backing off a step.

'I know exactly what you were doing, mate.' The smile on Callum's lips was benevolent, but the expression in his eyes made the younger man blanch. 'I suggest you lie in the bed of your own making and leave Georgina to lie in hers. Speaking of which, darling, I've managed to get us the last room available. You've had too much to drink and I'm not about to drive that death trap of yours.'

'But…' she began, alarm and outrage in her eyes.

'You don't need to be in work until Tuesday so why worry?'

'See you, Georgie,' Alex muttered, sliding away.

'Oh…what? Yes, sure.' To him their exchange must have seemed incredibly intimate. A light squabble between two lovers.

'Aren't you going to thank me for rescuing you? Or didn't the lady want to be rescued? Seducing the bridegroom on his wedding night might be the sort of revenge your soul craves.'

She was so angry that she felt as if she'd explode with frustration. 'My cravings are none of your business. How dare you interfere?' she breathed wrathfully. 'I can only hope your little contribution was pure fiction.'

He shrugged his broad shoulders. 'How had you intended getting home? You've been knocking back the vino with splendid abandon all afternoon.'

The way his eyes moved over her body as he said 'splendid abandon' made her head spin slightly and she didn't think 'vino' had anything to do with her reaction. 'I can't afford this place,' she said in a hushed tone. The rather over-the-top grandeur of the establishment was not to her taste and she was sure the prices were even less so.

'Don't worry, I'll pay.'

'You seem to be very affluent all of a sudden,' she said with suspicion.

'Well, at least you've not objected to spending the night with me,' he said, pleased to see the distrust swallowed up by horror.

'I have no intention of spending the night with you. I'll spend the night with Mother.'

'Who left a little earlier...and she wasn't alone. You might not be welcome there.'

She swallowed, admitting the accuracy of his surmise. 'How did you *know* I don't need to be in work till Tuesday?' she said, suddenly realising a point that had been niggling at the back of her mind.

'You must have told me,' he said carelessly. 'Whilst you were elaborating on your amazingly responsible position.'

She sucked in her breath wrathfully. The faint curl of disdain on his lips made her stiffen. 'I wasn't aware I said anything of the sort. You seem doubtful that I'm capable of working.'

He shrugged. 'It depends on how far you got due to your pretty face.'

Now she knew he was being sarcastic; pretty was one thing her face was not! 'I got where I am due to my own merits and a bit of luck. Much like anyone else, irrespective of sex. Just because you rely on your looks and dubious charm, don't assume we're all tarred with the same brush.'

'From what you said, your boss took a bit of a shine to you. I suppose your high-flown morals didn't let you take advantage of the fact?' he responded drily.

'Oliver merely gave me an opportunity to prove myself,' she said stiffly. The idea of Oliver being influenced by anyone or anything beyond his precious company was laughable. 'But if his successor has the same biased outlook as you I probably will be out on my ear shortly. I would imagine he'll be advised to do just that,' she admitted, a frown pleating her smooth brow.

On paper her credentials were not impressive and she seriously doubted whether she'd have the opportunity to prove her worth. There were several senior executives who had resented the responsibility Oliver had given her and they'd probably already fed the nephew from the outback enough to poison her chances of staying on.

Back-stabbing was an art form in the advertising world and she'd already suffered a good deal of spiteful innuendo concerning her promotion to Oliver's right hand. He might have been past middle age but he had been virile and active enough to give the scandalmongers fuel for their fantasies.

'Won't you get a fair hearing?' Callum asked, his expression hard and assessing as he watched the expressions flitting across her face.

She shrugged. 'The nephew is some farmer from the outback,' she observed dismissively. 'I doubt very much if he'll have an opinion of his own.' After Oliver's dynamic, hands-on management style she doubted if anything was ever going to be the same again.

'Still, you could hold his hand and make yourself as indispensable as you did to the uncle.'

The soft voice held a strange underlying acid note that made her eyes narrow and look beyond the languid air of casual interest. The blue eyes gazed back at her benignly, his lips drooped at one corner in a lopsided smile; it was an expression that was somehow strangely familiar. She couldn't *quite* put her finger on it.

'I've no desire to hold anyone's hand and that goes for you too,' she said forcefully, her mind returning to her more immediate problems. 'I can't possibly spend the night with you.'

'Why not compromise? Sleep off your afternoon's excess and you can drive us back this evening.'

His simple statement made all her worries about imminent seduction suddenly seem foolish. She cursed her overreaction. Verbal sparring of a sexual nature was probably as mundane as discussing the weather to him. That was what he did—made lonely women feel attractive. Mortified, she felt her spine stiffen defensively. He was probably more worried about getting back to town as early as possible. She was, after all, just another job, like any other lonely woman.

'That sounds reasonable,' she said briskly. Pride brought her chin up to an aggressive angle. 'What will you do?' It was deeply embarrassing to think she'd convinced herself that he was actually interested in her.

'Sleep, if you've no objection,' he drawled. 'My body clock's still haywire. I've been out of the country.'

'You're Australian?' He nodded, a wing of dark hair flopping into his eye; he brushed it back impatiently and her imagination was captured again by the long, elegant shape of his hands and fingers.

She closed her eyes and shook her head; the whole procedure took seconds but it did help focus her thoughts. The southern hemisphere seemed to have played a large part in her life recently, what with Oliver's nephew coming from there too. She could have done without either!

'I'm sure we can come to a civilised arrangement. I'm very sorry to delay you,' she said formally. 'Perhaps you could arrange some coffee for me?' About time I started acting like the cool career woman I'm meant to be, she thought.

A dark brow shot up and he gave her a slow, sardonic stare. 'Miss Brisk Efficiency,' he drawled, preparing to move away. 'Perhaps, as I've fulfilled my contract, you should intersperse your commands with the odd please and thank-you.'

She flushed at the remonstrance and gritted her teeth resentfully. She knew she was overcompensating for her ridiculous behaviour earlier but she wasn't about to admit it to him.

She was still staring after Callum, reflecting that he was the most appalling man she'd ever met, when Harriet appeared with a rustle of silk at her side. The bride got right down to the subject which was making her lips quiver with temper.

'I might have known you'd try and ruin my day out of pure spite!'

The sheer inaccuracy of this statement temporarily robbed Georgina of speech. 'Why would I want to do that?' she said eventually, her tone meant to deflate what looked like a volatile situation. The last thing she needed right now was a scene.

'As if you didn't know. I suppose you don't know Alex hasn't taken his eyes off you.' The cold eyes swept disparagingly over Georgina's finery. 'You really don't have the figure to take that outfit.'

'Then I expect Alex is only marvelling at my bad taste,' Georgina responded, her temper wearing paper-thin by this point. 'You really have no need to worry, Harriet; I have no aspirations to take your husband from you. I'm not alone, in case you hadn't noticed.'

'What's wrong, Georgie—hasn't he found out yet you're frigid?' The blue eyes sparkled with malice as she gave a brittle laugh. 'Alex said it was like being in bed with a statue. I'm not worried about *you*,' she sneered. 'I just didn't want you to make a fool of yourself.' With a final, triumphant smile she swept away, her long skirts hissing on the floor.

Georgina was secretly amazed at how she'd managed to keep her own expression blank. Each poisonous dart had hit its target but she'd never let the other girl know. She could have told her that Alex had in fact slept with his new wife before her, but she didn't want to stoop to the same name-calling tactics as her cousin.

The timetable of events only made her own humiliation worse. It was ironic that when, after resisting Alex's attempts to make their relationship more intimate, she had finally felt she was ready he had already been unfaithful to her with Harriet. I gave my all and it obviously compared unfavourably with what he already had on offer, she thought with bitter self-mockery.

'You look pale. Are you all right?' Callum asked, returning with a cup of coffee.

'Sorry, did you say something?' she responded vaguely. It was hard to put the bitter recollections aside and concentrate on the present.

'The girlie chat with the blushing bride has left you looking like a basket case,' he observed bluntly.

'Well, I'm not about to share all the grisly contents with you,' she said, straightening her shoulders. 'So you'll have to settle for a coffee while I go and apply some blusher.'

Callum found himself admiring the determined set of her jaw and the ramrod line of her slender back as she wound her way through the throng. Whatever else she was, Georgina Campion had guts.

Georgina had had two cups of coffee, the bride was ready to leave and Georgina's head was splitting. They were all crammed in the foyer for the ritual send-off when Harriet deliberately caught her cousin's eye; the look of triumph was malicious. Recalling her encounter with Alex earlier, Georgina could almost feel sorry for her, with the emphasis on almost. She could certainly meet the stare with perfect equanimity—a fact that made Harriet's pretty features harden.

Georgina wondered what she had ever done to make the girl dislike her so much. She watched as Harriet's arm moved in an arc and the bouquet hit her full-force in the face, knocking her hat off in the process. The action brought a flurry of giggles and high-spirited comments. Georgina felt her eyes water with pain but smiled through the tears.

By the time Callum retrieved her hat it had been trampled on. She was clutching the rather limp flowers unenthusiastically as he dusted it down and handed it back to her. He watched the narrow-eyed, dispassionate intensity as she brushed a stray tear from her watering eyes.

'There goes a week's pay,' she observed, dropping it in the nearest waste-paper bin. She didn't need any reminders of this day.

'Georgie, can we offer you two a lift anywhere? Your mother's?' Uncle George included Callum in the good-natured offer.

'We have a room actually, but thanks anyway,' Callum said, speaking for them. She felt the weight of his hands once more on her slumped shoulders, wielding the strength of tensile steel as they rested deceptively lightly upon her.

'I think you can drop the role now,' she snapped as her uncle moved away with an affectionate admonition not to be a stranger. 'You've more than fulfilled your obligations. On second thoughts your last official duty can be to get rid of these.' Her nose wrinkled in distaste as she pushed the bouquet into his hands.

'Aren't they supposed to predict your imminent nuptials?' he said, flicking a white rose with his finger.

'Not if I'm conscious,' she said feelingly.

'I think that's called tempting fate, Georgie.' He drawled the hated appellation with deliberate relish. 'Or should I revert to Miss Campion now my role as official escort is over?'

'You could revert to silence,' she suggested, eyeing her tall, elegant companion with grim dislike.

'Feeling hung-over, are we?'

'I don't suppose *you* drank anything?' she snapped sarcastically.

'Nothing alcoholic,' he agreed. 'After long-haul flying that would have been a mistake. You're one of my first...' he raised his eyes and she saw he looked peculiarly amused '...assignments since I arrived.'

'I thought you'd be one of those macho types convinced their iron constitution can withstand anything. Or are you a fitness freak?'

'You're smarting, but don't take your frustrations out on me. I'm not renowned for being the suffer-in-silence type.'

She gave a loud sniff. 'I can imagine what you're renowned for,' she snapped nastily.

He caught hold of her arm as she stalked past him. 'And what would that be?' he enquired silkily.

She looked pointedly at his fingers on the fabric of her sleeve. 'Gigolo,' she accused, choosing her words rashly.

His rather grim expression froze for a moment before it thawed and deep laughter rumbled from the region of his chest. Laughter that was quite distressingly attractive— deep, vibrant and uninhibited.

'When you get all sanctimonious and holier-than-thou your mouth turns down at the corners,' he observed as his mirth died away. 'Like this,' he added in a spirit of helpfulness, and he touched his thumbs to the corners of her mouth. 'Mind you, I'm flattered you think I have the credentials.'

She'd been going to apologise for the rash accusation, which she had regretted the instant it had left her lips, but his totally unexpected response had taken her aback. The touch against her mouth made her draw a startled breath. Then as her glance flicked upwards she caught a stark expression in his half-closed eyes which evaporated so swiftly that she decided it had been a figment of her rampant imagination. I must keep a tighter rein on these erotic fantasies, she concluded.

'I've had an awful day and I can do without any more helpful hints from you,' she snapped from between clenched teeth. 'Do you suppose anyone would notice if I slipped away?'

'I'm sure everyone will notice when *we* slip away,' he replied, looking around the room with its thinning crowd of revellers. 'But that will only reinforce your role as fulfilled woman of the nineties, won't it?'

She hated the sarcasm in his deep voice even more than the heat which scorched across her skin. 'People's prejudices are not my fault.'

'When you go out of your way to perpetuate them they are,' he returned imperturbably. 'Shall we go and make our thank-yous to our hosts?' he suggested, watching her choke on her indignation with a faint smile calculated to inflame her wrath.

*   *   *

The room had nothing to distinguish it from any other in the establishment. It was luxurious and impersonal. Georgina sponged her hands and face, slid off her shoes and lay on the bed, her eyes half-closed. Through the slits she watched Callum stretch himself out on the sofa which was far too short to accommodate his length. Logically she should have offered him the bed, but she kept her lips firmly closed. A bit of discomfort might do him some good, she thought with unwonted viciousness.

'I just need a nap,' she said instead, stifling a yawn. The day had been more mentally stressful than she had anticipated. Coping with the emotional impact had been even more traumatic than she had imagined. The wine might have helped deaden the pain, but it did have its side-effects, she admitted ruefully as her eyes, feeling leaden-weighted, closed completely.

It occurred to her that she was being incredibly trusting, locking herself in a room with a man who was almost a total stranger and whom she instinctively didn't trust. Strangely it didn't occur to her that he would take advantage of the situation. Quite peacefully she drifted into sleep and didn't feel the cover being gently pulled over her.

CHAPTER FOUR

GEORGINA AWOKE to total darkness. Her mind slowly cleared as her eyes accustomed themselves to the darkness. With an exclamation she sat bolt upright, as if a light bulb in her brain had suddenly been switched on. God, what time was it? Why hadn't Callum woken her?

Georgina scrabbled for the light switch on the wall beside her. She made contact with the small reading light and the room was softly illuminated. She picked up her discarded watch and, squinting, read two-thirty. She grimaced and let out another groan. The entire room was a blur: her contact lenses lay in their container in the bathroom where she'd removed them.

She swung her sleep-stiffened limbs over the side of the bed and ran her fingers through her tousled hair. The sound of deep, steady breathing on the other side of the room indicated that her companion was still asleep. She'd soon alter that! Barefooted, she padded across the room.

'Callum.' She said the name softly. Instinctively she'd been inclined to blame him for the unintended stopover; now she could see that that was uncharitable. He was clearly exhausted; he hadn't moved an inch since she'd noisily awoken.

One arm was flung over his head and the angular planes of his face looked less sharply defined in sleep, making him appear younger, but that could be the effect of her short-sightedness. The jacket he'd draped over himself had slid in a crumpled heap to the floor.

She took a step nearer and tripped over his shoes. She just managed to stop herself falling on top of him. On her knees she caught her breath as the outline of his body, the closeness made her freeze.

Wake the man and stop staring at him like a witless idiot, she told herself firmly. Sympathy for his exhaustion was an emotion severely misplaced under the circumstances. And sympathy didn't cover the range of emotions she was experiencing, but she stubbornly refused to recognise that.

'Callum!' Mouth near his ear, she called his name firmly. She pulled back, expecting to see him jolt upright, but, other than a faint flicker of his eyelids, he didn't move. 'Callum, it's late.' This time the decibels were not gentle. With disbelief she watched him turn on his side; this man doesn't sleep, he dies! she thought with frustration.

'Callum, wake up—now!' Still kneeling beside the sofa, she shook his shoulder. If he didn't come to soon she would leave him stranded, she decided, and serve him right. She didn't pause to examine the origin of her intense antagonism. The grunts she had in response were quite encouraging. 'Wake up; it's two-thirty,' she persisted. She gave a sigh of relief when he rolled over towards her. His eyes were open slightly, unfocused, but at least he was awake.

Georgina's relief slid away when she saw the glazed expression in his half-closed eyes. It was scorchingly hot and slumbrously sexy, immobilising her as firmly as an iron hand. She wasn't even sure he was seeing her. Was he still partly in a world of dreams where boundaries were only limited by the imagination? Blood began to pump fiercely in her ears, throbbing in time to her accelerated heart rate.

Before his eyes moved downwards she thought she glimpsed that strange recognition in them that had been there when they had met. She certainly felt the unfamiliar tug at her senses.

She realised belatedly that during her sleep the two top buttons of her jacket had come adrift. Following the direction of his gaze, she saw that the gaping lapels had fallen open to reveal the silky, lace-trimmed peach camisole she wore. It ended just above the indentation of her navel, a fact that was revealed when he lifted one capable hand to flick open the bottom two buttons of the jacket. The deep, growling sigh of appreciation made her raise her dazed eyes to his face; the fine hair on the nape of her neck had stood on end at the basic sound of primal pleasure.

'Callum, it's late. We...we've overslept.' With a gasp her head fell back and her words dissolved into a dry-throated sigh as one hand in the small of her back pulled her closer and his mouth moved to the hardened tip of one swollen breast. The silky fabric moved to one side as he fastened onto the searingly sensitive area; his tongue and teeth nuzzled and tugged at the sensitive flesh. The roughness on his chin grazed her silky, smooth skin.

Invisible pathways sent the flaming sensation to the deepest portion of her belly, contracting the muscles in a series of mind-blowing quivers. The heat exploding inside her sent a hot flush over her entire body. One section of her mind was aware that this man was taking unbelievable liberties and another that she didn't want him to stop.

This was wildly irresponsible and she'd begin to regret this weakness bitterly soon, she told herself, but at that moment the craving to expand on these sensations was too great to deny.

'Stop it!' The strangled plea emerged from her internal struggle. Hands on his shoulders, she pushed against him, bracing her elbows to make her rejection felt.

The feeling of loss when he lifted his head was so intense that she was unprepared to disguise her response. It spilled out of her, reflected in the deep frustration that shone in her eyes.

His eyes holding hers, she watched him regain his shredded control. The glazed expression receded slightly but his eyes still burnt with a barely damped down passion. The way the muscles in his neck contracted and strained gave some indication that the withdrawal had not been accomplished easily.

'Why?' he asked, after a long, heavy silence.

His question flustered her even further and the slight rasp in his deep voice made her shiver. Her hands were still firmly against his shoulders as she knelt beside him. Even though he could have brushed aside her protests she instinctively knew he wouldn't.

I ought to move them, she thought, looking at her splayed fingers outlined against the fabric of his shirt. She could feel the sinewed hardness of the muscle underneath the light covering, and the sensation of power in repose was terrifyingly addictive. Her fingers moved and the motion became perilously close to a caress as she was unable to break the contact.

'Why...?' she echoed faintly, her stunned brain having lost track of the conversation. She ought to have been able to come up with several answers to that one.

'Why do you want me to stop?'

The dark shadow of growth along his jaw emphasised the hollows of his prominent cheekbones and gave him a faintly piratical look. He swung his long legs over the side of the substitute bed.

There were several hundred very good reasons but somehow her tongue would formulate none. The sensual craving was singing through her veins, defeating every fibre of common sense she possessed. 'We can't spend the night here,' she said, frustrated that this very obvious fact seemed to be escaping him.

'At this precise moment I can't think of anything better to do.'

'You mean sex,' she said, almost achieving the pragmatic note she sought. 'You were asleep,' she said, with a faint laugh that was meant to close the subject. 'I won't hold you responsible for anything you did then.' With an enormous effort her hands moved but, as if to prolong the contact, they slid down his arms slowly.

Her sensitive fingertips memorised the bulge of biceps and the sinewed curve of his hair-sprinkled forearms. A look of intense concentration spread over her face as she caught her tongue between her teeth. At the termination of the journey, as her fingers slid over the backs of his hands, he suddenly raised his arms to either side and with a sharp flick turned his wrists. Palm to palm, their hands touched and his fingers firmly interlaced with hers.

'I emerged from sleep to find soft, inviting curves tantalisingly within my grasp. I acted on a physical response that most healthy males would exhibit but I wasn't asleep. I'm *not* asleep...' His voice trailed away as his eyes dropped to the contours of her breasts, which were lifted and thrust forward by the elevation of her arms. The slight pressure of his curling fingers stopped her pulling free to cover herself.

'Not acting on physical responses is what raises us...most of us...above the beasts in the field.'

'Don't mistake basic instinct for something vulgar or sordid, Georgina.' He harshly foiled her attempt to break the sensual bonds. 'Sometimes you should just trust yourself to instinct. Your instinct has been screaming out from the instant you saw me.'

'It's late; we should leave...' she faltered, trying hard

to fight the debilitating weakness that coiled in her belly waiting to escape.

The breathy sound of her voice made her wince. This man made her breathless; she ought to be angry at his confident claim but it was achingly true and part of her longed to acknowledge the fact. This was far more than a simple if powerful physical response; there had been some part of her that had recognised, been drawn to something in him from the moment she had laid eyes on him. Her instinctive aggression had been partly a defence mechanism.

She'd never experienced this deep, primeval craving for Alex's lovemaking. Yet this relative stranger, who was nothing to her, could make her ache. A soft sound of distress and confusion escaped the confines of her throat.

'The moment I saw your hair fall down your back like a river of warm fire I wanted to see it against your bare flesh.'

The husky admission made her lick her dry lips, her wide eyes fixed on his face. He lowered her arms and placed her hands against his chest; she could feel the rhythm of his breathing, sense the blood running just below the surface. The vitality in him was almost contagious; he was more *alive* than anyone she'd ever met. Carefully, his eyes still on her face, he slid her jacket off her shoulders.

Georgina closed her eyes, trembling as the fine hairs on her arms stood on end. He was unveiling her with a sensitivity that was almost painful in its precision.

At first, when Alex had left her bitter, her illusions shattered, she had toyed with the idea of seducing someone— a childish act of revenge she would have flaunted in front of Alex's nose. She had soon seen the flaws in this desperate need to hit out and had been ashamed of the impulse. Today had been a more dignified way of showing him that her heart was not broken, that there was life after Alex!

But *this* wasn't part of any plan! What had she told Callum? That she had rejected emotions? If that *was* true how was she able to *feel* so intensely at the moment? She had never experienced feelings approaching this emotional depth in her life.

The thoughts flickered through her head in a fraction of a second. Callum was stroking her hair, feeling the crackle of static as his hand ran over the burnished mane which fell to her waist.

'Do you really want me to stop, Georgina? Do you?' he persisted, placing a finger under her chin and tilting her head upwards. His sexuality had an insolence that should have repelled her but she felt something in her rising to the challenge.

'No, I don't.' Her voice was oddly composed. Relief, deep and profound, flooded through her.

A nerve in his left cheek leapt and the tension in him didn't relax; he betrayed no smug satisfaction. The muscles in his lean frame seemed to tighten. 'Be sure about this.' It was half a warning and she shivered.

'I am.' Strangely, she was. She'd never felt more certain about anything seeming right in her life.

'Are you using me to get back at your ex?' Once more his perception was uncomfortably penetrating and her colour rose because she had once been capable of plotting such pettiness.

'Would it matter?' she asked, angry because now that she had made her decision she didn't want her motives questioned. How could she reply when her motives were a mystery to her too? Something primal and instinctual had taken over. But one thing she did know was that revenge was not part of it.

'Later, maybe, but now now,' he said obscurely, his lips

twisting in a strange, savage smile. He stood upright, pulling her with him. Her legs felt weak and insubstantial as she leant heavily on him. The enormity of what she was doing blanked out all other thoughts for a second and with eyes dark with conflict she raised her face and looked him in the eye.

Callum made a hoarse sound in his throat and picked her up as if she weighed nothing. She was breaking every rule she'd ever thought governed her life but it felt so good to wind her arms around his neck and tuck her head under the angle of his jaw.

His eyes stayed on her as he laid her on the bed and undressed her slowly, the movements of his beautiful hands oddly mesmerising. She felt the air against her flesh and saw herself reflected in his eyes. The experience was overwhelming. Tears, hot and scalding, stung the back of her eyelids. Her throat ached with emotion; the slowness was a strange form of torture. Her senses had reached screaming pitch. Was this his way of giving her time to change her mind?

Then as she looked into his eyes she saw he had already gone past the point where choice entered into it. He looked driven—that was the only way she could think of describing the glow in those incredible blue depths. And when he finally touched her, not with the gentle whispers of sensation that he'd employed as he'd undressed her, but laying his hands on her skin possessively, with intimate knowledge of how and where to caress her, she lost the power to think. In his hands she became a creature of molten fire.

The eye of the storm had passed and a fierce desperation seemed to possess him. He lowered his head, his mouth covering hers. He drank as if he'd drain her of life. When he raised his head she could feel the deep shudders that racked his lean body. She welcomed the feverish rain of kisses, soft bites and the intimate exploration that exposed every nerve-ending in her body to him.

Her hunger to touch him was just as uncontrolled. His skin beneath her fingers was warm satin; the salty tang of it made her moan as her tongue darted out to taste more. His superior strength didn't give rise to any fear; it only excited and drove her deeper into the sensual maelstrom that possessed her.

Colour highlighted the high contours of his cheekbones as her hands followed her eyes over the animal grace of his body. The mixture of awe and sultry passion in her eyes intensified the savage exhilaration that smouldered in his own.

'Are you pleased to see how much I want you?' he growled. The sensually lazy smile on his lips slipped as her mouth explored one flat, pebble-hard masculine nipple. He gave a strangled moan and his hands sank deep into the luxuriant thickness of her hair to cradle her skull.

Her body arched in a sensuous, almost feline gesture of pleasure as her hands slid up to his shoulders. 'I enjoy looking at you,' she admitted without a trace of self-consciousness.

With Alex there had been that awful self-conscious embarrassment. After waiting so long she'd felt strangely cheated and disillusioned. If Harriet was to be believed, so had Alex. But now was no time for the past; somehow, just looking at Callum made her lose the inhibitions she'd imagined were an integral part of her personality. The scent of his arousal, the texture of his skin—she was intoxicated by the sensual bombardment and greedy to glut her starved senses.

He passively accepted her voyage of discovery for a few moments before a hoarse sound of denial emerged from between his clenched teeth. With a dexterity that left her breathless and suffering from a mixture of frustration and soaring anticipation he flipped her over onto her back.

'I enjoy looking at you too.' He repeated her words throatily as his eyes roamed hungrily over her supine form. Her skin under his probing fingers was satin-smooth and damp and hot. He felt the fine, delicate network of muscles under the satiny surface contract responsively under his touch.

Her body was wide open to him, boneless, yet gripped by the fierce tension that pulsed through her. 'Please, Callum...I can't bear...I need...' Her voice was strained beyond recognition as she ran her hands along his sweat-slick skin and felt the febrile shudder that racked his powerful torso.

He lay above her, suspended on his elbows, close but not nearly close enough. His thighs rested against her hips as he settled against her spread-eagled body. She felt him swallow a strangled groan and heard the grating of his teeth as her questing hands slid lower, seeking the velvet-sheathed hardness. When he kissed her fiercely she could taste the blood on his tongue.

He lifted her hips upwards to meet him and as she closed her eyes the image imprinted on her brain was of his face, the lines etched with tension and a wild, fierce triumph.

It had hurt with Alex and she was sure it would now; she'd been awed by the pulsating size of Callum. Her eyes opened wide with pleasurable shock as her body expanded to absorb him painlessly and the last remnants of apprehension slipped away. She felt exultant! She could follow where he led and she did, climbing higher and higher. The pulsating rhythm flowed through her and she felt indivisible from the man who filled her.

The first ripple of a fierce contraction hit her seconds before the primitive cry was torn from deep within his chest. Aftershocks still shook her when his weight lifted from her and his head slid down to nestle against her breast. He was still stroking the smooth curve of her thigh and behind when he finally fell asleep.

There had been no word, just one moment when his heavy-lidded eyes had sought out her own languorous glance. There had been a question there which she'd been too stunned to interpret.

The muscles in her body might have relaxed but her mind was firing on all cylinders as she cradled the powerful body spread out against her.

A solid lump of emotion throbbed in her throat as she eased herself from under his constricting weight. She couldn't regret anything that had been so perfect and fulfilling in a way she hadn't dreamt was possible. Making love with Alex had left her feeling empty and disillusioned; she would always be grateful to this man for teaching her that it didn't have to be that way.

What had it been to him? Her hand went up to cover her quivering mouth. Sensitive and generous he might have been, but to him she would only ever be a one-night stand. It was brutal but necessary for her to face the truth. The awkwardness of the morning after would ruin the magical memory. She couldn't expect him to share her wonder. She didn't want to see the night through his eyes and have it made sordid and superficial.

She had no intention of confusing generous, skilful lovemaking with affection and warmth. The irony of it! She who had despised her own mother's weaknesses had succumbed to the very same primitive urges she had condemned. She felt guilty when she thought of how self-righteous she had been in the past.

Quietly she slipped into her clothes. She didn't want his affection, his love; her mind balked at the word and the accompanying surge of craving that was physically painful in its intensity. He was a stranger who had by some perversity of destiny been the only man she'd ever met who could fill her with the mindless compulsion. Perhaps a secret part of her had accepted the inevitability of this in the first few seconds of seeing him.

Her eyes watered as she slipped her contact lenses in and blinked at her image in the bathroom mirror. 'She who loves and runs away lives to…love?' The idea of such intimacy with another man made her grimace in protest. She'd crammed her wild, reckless moments into one night, she decided shakily, not quite meeting the wide eyes of the girl in the mirror.

She kept brushing tears from her cheeks as she drove along dark, quiet roads. What would he feel when he awoke to find himself alone? Relief? Annoyance? Probably a mixture of the two, she decided, sniffing stoically. She had made sure she had settled the hotel bill even though it was going to mean a tight budget for the next month.

CHAPTER FIVE

GEORGINA WAS BACK at the office on Tuesday. Glancing at her reflection in the glass-fronted office wall as she walked confidently past, she was pleased to see that no hint of the weekend's events showed in her appearance.

The tailored black suit was one of the several she wore to work; its mid-calf-length skirt was as modest and un-challenging as the cream silk shirt she wore buttoned up to the neck. Her hair was wound into a tight knot on the nape of her neck and a pair of round-framed spectacles was perched on her nose in preference to her contact lenses.

After several unsuccessful job interviews she had opted for a change of image; how much this had contributed to her gaining her present job she wasn't sure, but it helped keep most potential office Romeos at bay—that and a rep-utation for having an abrasive tongue guaranteed to deflate male egos at twenty paces.

The one time in her life she had trusted a man he had let her down. Before the weekend she had been confident of her ability never to permit herself to be in that position again. She banished the disquiet that thoughts of the week-end gave her and placed an expression of firm determi-nation on her troubled features. The girl in the pink suit belonged to another world; if she tried very hard she could *almost* believe she didn't exist.

'The new boss is in.' The competent secretary with whom she had originally had a spiky relationship looked

uncharacteristically excited. Georgina could easily understand the antagonism and suspicion the older woman had
felt towards the young girl who had leap-frogged straight
from a lowly clerical post to the heady heights of PA.

Georgina had worked hard to prove her worth and had
been frank about her need to learn from her colleague's
experience. Mary Webb had reserved her judgement but
had been won over eventually by the sheer determination
the young girl displayed. Unlike her predecessor Georgina
never took credit for anything she hadn't been responsible
for. Their working relationship was now warmly friendly.

'What's he like?' Georgina asked, wondering just how
out of depth this farmer was after one day at the helm.
'Do you think he's going to try and step into Oliver's
shoes?'

Mary shrugged. 'Shall we just say he's electrified the
workforce, my dear? And the sight of dignified executives
all prepared to turn cartwheels to gain a Brownie point is
unsettling, but I quite like it.'

Georgina felt her slightly scornful smile slip. 'You mean
he's not a naïve farmer with straw behind his ears?' That'll
teach me to make snap judgements, she thought, an iron-
ical light illuminating her eyes. I should have had more
faith in Oliver's judgement, she chided herself.

'Let Miss Campion judge for herself. I'm ready for her
now.'

Mary struck the heel of her hand to her head and grimaced at the intercom on her desk. She mimed a desperate
apology to her friend who had gone several shades paler
than normal.

Georgina shook her head understandingly and wished
she hadn't opened her mouth. First impressions were incredibly important and she'd just made the sort of impact
she'd have preferred not to. She took a deep breath and

whispered, 'Wish me luck,' before knocking smartly on the door and entering with more confidence than she felt.

The wide floor-length window had a view over the city that drew the eyes of anyone entering the room. The panorama was, however, lost on Georgina; a figure with his back to her was deep in apparent contemplation of the vista.

Broad-shouldered and lean-hipped, he stood well over six feet tall. The loose-fitting Italian suit didn't disguise the fact that this man was at the height of his physical powers. Georgina didn't need him to turn around to know he was in his early thirties; she even knew the colour of his eyes.

The room tilted slightly as she gasped for air, tiny black dots danced across her vision, and a sound like the sea roared in her ears. Confusion, disbelief and a sort of numb dread stole over her simultaneously. What she was seeing was impossible. Hallucination? Had he made such an awesome impact upon her that she was going to see his face and figure everywhere?

He turned around and the last remnants of colour seeped from her clammy skin. All the classic symptoms of shock, she told herself as a bubble of hysteria rose in her throat.

'Good morning, Miss Campion.' The soft voice was no hallucination; neither was the brilliant, icy stare.

'Who *are* you?'

'Have a seat,' he said, walking around to the other side of the vast, leather-topped desk. He pushed a chair behind her legs and her shaking knees collapsed as she sank into it.

'The escort company didn't send you?'

'I can see how you've progressed so rapidly, with that sort of amazing mental capability.'

'You let me think…think…'

He'd made a fool of her so completely that she could

hardly grasp the full implications. He knew more about her... He'd cold-bloodedly seduced her and she had fallen like a ripe... A sound of denial escaped her lips and she clenched her hands into two tight fists. Over the past forty-eight hours she'd grown to despise her lack of self-control, and her inability to resist the primitive need that had sent her into Callum's arms. Now she also felt sick to the core at having her vulnerability exposed to those ruthless blue eyes. This was her reward for abandoning all her idealism and principles for a shallow interlude of intense pleasure.

'*You* told me who I was,' he corrected her. 'You could say I did you a favour. If I hadn't appeared so fortuitously what would you have done? I arrived wanting nothing more than to know why you apparently know more about certain accounts than very senior executives. It seemed amazing that the absence of a PA could virtually immobilise a firm of this size.

'Did you know your phone is out of order, incidentally?' he asked, flicking an invisible speck off his immaculate jacket. 'It occurred to me I might get more insight into a devious character capable of manipulating a shrew old fox like Oliver by going along with your little deception.' He sounded neither apologetic nor ashamed of his actions and Georgina felt the lick of pure rage race through her shaking body.

'And did you get much insight?' she asked in a small, hard voice that was by now quite steady.

'I got quite a lot more than I'd bargained for.'

With a gasp she shot to her feet; his implication had been unmistakable. 'If we're talking manipulation,' she yelled, twin flags of colour blooming on the crests of her cheekbones, 'you're a regular con merchant, Mr Stewart.'

'So you know who I am now. Considering I left my bush hat back home, I'm impressed.' The creases around his eyes deepened but his narrowed eyes betrayed no hu-

mour. 'Which is more, if I recall, than you are with my
capabilities of running this *vast* empire.' He drawled the
term with languid scorn. 'As we're on such...intimate
terms, Georgina, perhaps you should make it Callum.'

The degradation seemed to fuse into a solid mass behind
her breastbone; the tightness made it hard to breathe. 'Under the circumstances, Mr Stewart, I'm sure you'll accept
my resignation.' The firm, steady voice seemed to be coming from a long way off.

A faint spasm moved the sensual line of his lips. The
despicable rat was really enjoying the joke! 'At a future
date, Georgina, I shall be delighted, but I never mix business with pleasure. Your contract requires that you give
six weeks' notice and if you walk out prior to that date I
shall sue you. I shall also see to it that you don't get a
comparable job. Possibly no job at all,' he mused thoughtfully; his eyes, unlike his voice, were neither languid nor
casual.

These dire and casually voiced threats made very little
impression on the panic that surged through her; the urge
to run was sending heart-racing adrenaline flooding
through her veins. 'I can't work with you.' Walking
through fire seemed a much more appealing prospect!

'Certainly not,' he observed coolly. 'But you *do* and
shall work *for* me.' He watched the flush mount her cheeks
as this barb penetrated. 'Several of the firm's major con-
tracts—the lifeblood, so to speak—were Oliver's personal
pets. There appears to be no physical evidence concerning
the ongoing campaigns—no notes, no computer files.'

His eyes bored into her as though the entire responsibility for this situation rested on her shoulders. Indignation
made her straighten those slender attributes.

'The customers' confidence and loyalty appear to be dis-
solving rapidly,' he continued drily. 'When I can't produce
a senior executive capable of allaying their fears I can't

really blame them. When making the sort of financial commitment they are, they're entitled to expect something tangible.'

'You might be able to sit at Oliver's desk but I can't be held responsible if you can't fill his shoes,' she replied, managing a faint, derogatory smirk. This was a nightmare and any moment now she was going to wake up!

No man was ever going to use her...not after Alex's betrayal. Had she ever felt that confident? Callum Stewart had manipulated her in the most coldly callous way imaginable. Her eyes glimmered with loathing as she vowed he'd never realise just how deeply he'd punctured her emotional defences. The loathing that seethed like poison in her veins was equally divided between herself and him.

All her smug confidence, accumulated over years of retaining her virtue, had been demolished by short-term exposure to this demon. Even the humiliation of finding out Alex's shortcomings didn't rate compared with the humiliation she felt now.

Callum lowered his lean frame into the chair behind the impressive desk—a desk that might have made some men look insignificant—but it was to him that eyes were drawn, not the furniture.

'Oliver and I were not well acquainted; he was my mother's brother and she has never felt inclined to be tied down by emotional attachment. Call it a family trait,' he observed, with an edge to his voice that she couldn't interpret. 'You and she have a good deal in common,' he remarked, his nostrils flaring with obvious distaste. 'And I don't go in for displays of false sentiment. I'm glad to hear you were very fond of him,' he drawled sarcastically. 'As he obviously was of you. Straight from a clerical job to indispensable right hand to the man himself. Quite a quantum leap...'

She got to her feet, head held high. 'I don't have to

listen to any more nasty innuendoes from you. I earned my salary.'

'You don't need to sell yourself to me, Georgina; I've already discovered your talents.'

Her high colour faded dramatically, leaving her paper-white. 'I didn't sleep my way to my position, despite what the grapevine likes to imply.' Oliver had interviewed her out of curiosity, he'd told her later; his interest had been piqued by the sheer gall of a junior clerk applying for the position of PA to the company chairman. She'd sold herself, but not in the way everyone liked to think.

'What a pity you didn't know my true identity before you slipped into my bed.'

'To be accurate, it was *my* bed.'

'If you hadn't thought I was penniless I imagine it might have taken a lot more persuasion to get you between the sheets, whoever they belonged to. You must be kicking yourself when you think about all the things you might have extracted from me before you came up with the goods. Who knows? You might have thought I even rated your being there in the morning.'

He was on his feet now and when he moved the illusion of safety which the desk had given her disappeared. It took all her stubborn determination not to step backwards away from his advancing figure.

'You're the sort of woman who manipulates men by withholding your favours until you get what you want, aren't you, Georgina? The wholesome, wide-eyed appeal overlying the sultry promise, you're all promise and no fulfilment under normal circumstances. You obviously satisfy your very physical nature like any cat on heat does, with the occasional stranger.'

'You're disgusting!' She was shaking in response to his cold character assassination. It was all too easy to see how he'd reached his conclusions and, short of revealing herself as a naïve idiot, she didn't see how she could convince him otherwise. And she didn't owe him any explanations.

'Did the boyfriend get tired of you sleeping your way to the top?' The false sympathy made her jaw ache with tension. 'Or did he approve of your methods? Was it just your taste for anonymous one-night stands he couldn't stomach? Only it's not anonymous after all...is it, Georgina?'

'I hate you!' Her voice shook with a solid depth of emotion. He was insulting and humiliating her past the point she had imagined endurable. It occurred to her that Alex would stare to hear her spoken of as some sort of *femme fatale* when ironically he had given her second place in his test run for perfect wife material.

'Because I know you for what you are. Behind that wide-eyed simpering act you're solely motivated by ambition, aren't you?' His voice was expressionless but the anger that glittered in his eyes reverberated through her like a scream. 'Personal relationships take second place to that. You sacrificed your prospective marriage to that.'

'My marriage and my personal life are none of your business.' A thin white line of rage outlined his sculpted lips and she found herself unable to drag her eyes from the detail.

'Did you have it in mind when you hired an escort?' He met her stormy glare with a smile of smooth contempt. 'Ending up in a hotel room to satisfy the appetites that sleeping with men old enough to be your father can't assuage?'

Callum was containing his anger with enormous difficulty. He'd planned to conduct this interview with cold disdain but seeing her again had made him forget everything except the fact that he'd allowed crude, sexual hunger to override his prime rule never to let his emotions get out of control. He'd actually reached a point where he'd convinced himself she wasn't the hard, conniving little tramp he'd taken her for.

In retrospect, he could see he'd only believed what he'd wanted to believe to justify his own weakness. Waking up to find a cold place beside him in the bed had revealed all too clearly how shallow her involvement had been! He'd let his libido take over from logic and he couldn't forgive the weakness or the cause of it.

He'd been going to order her off the premises, but the moment she'd suggested she go he'd instantly decided to do just the opposite. He'd make her time as uncomfortable as was in his power. The next time *he* was going to be the one doing the walking out.

After the sound of her hand striking his face there was only the noise of her own laboured breathing in the room.

After a second Callum raised his hand experimentally to his jaw and touched the reddened patch. 'Don't try that again.' The sound of divine retribution was in his voice.

'I hope never to be in the same room as you again, so hopefully the opportunity won't arise.' Her voice shook as much as her body.

'So the fierce dedication to Mallory's expires once the boss is not blinded by your little act. Nice to know Oliver's confidence in you was so totally misplaced. Inside your head,' he continued, stepping forward and unexpectedly pressing his hands to either side of her skull, 'are details that could mean the difference between prosperity and liquidation.'

Her head in a vice-like grip, Georgina had no option but to meet his challenging stare head-on. The pugnacious expression in her eyes glazed over as the sexual charge of his nearness began to make itself felt above the antagonism and conflict. The ripples of warm, insidious heat curling across her nerve-endings were as terrifying as they were hypnotic.

'I think you're overstating matters.' If it was true—and, knowing how unorthodox Oliver had been, it was just possible, she conceded—could she walk out on him? The firm had meant everything to Oliver, and after the opportunities he'd given her didn't she owe him something? Could she let his life's work vanish? 'You're not appealing to my better nature, are you? I thought I didn't have one.' The bitterness in her voice made his expression grow sardonic.

He released her so swiftly that she almost lost her balance. He picked an envelope up off the desk and shook it in front of her nose. 'If you leave us in the lurch you'll effectively be making this little lot worth a fraction of its value.'

She stared at him blankly.

'I suppose you don't know what's in here?' His lip curled scornfully as he sat against the desk, his long legs spread out before him, feet braced in the inches-deep Aubusson carpet. Her confused expression seemed to irritate him. 'As you know, you weren't mentioned in the will.'

'I never expected to be—'

'However—' his interruption sliced through her protest '—I was charged to deliver this bequest personally—and I place the emphasis on *personally*—to you. Unorthodox, but very Oliver.'

She stared at the brown paper package and instinctively placed her hands behind her back. 'I don't know—' she began half-fearfully before the explosive sound from his throat cut her off. 'Humour me and tell me what's in it.'

'Oliver valued your services to the tune of one hundred grand's worth of shares.'

'That's not p-possible.'

'I love the husky little catch; despite my better judgement I want to kiss the hurt better.'

Still frozen with disbelief, she raised her eyes from the

envelope to his face. The angry contempt on it seemed aimed at himself—a fact that only increased her confusion.

'If you want it, come and get it,' he said suddenly, and the rush of words had less of an authoritative ring to them. There was challenge, but there was also husky appeal.

'I don't want it.'

'But I want you.' The words emerged through a fog of anger. To her spinning head he seemed to move in slow motion as he reached out a hand and she saw her own clasped within it. She didn't try to resist the pressure that drew her closer until she stood within the V of his thighs. She was face to face with him at this level. Her face contorted in near agony as the exquisite torture of the intimate contact and instant knowledge of his desire lanced through her body.

Memories she'd spent the last two days trying to file away in rational order flamed into violent life; hunger she'd vowed never to experience again soared like a bird. The vows were doubly important now but she still couldn't catch hold of them. Her body ached and throbbed. He was not the casual stranger who was enticingly attractive, he was a dangerous, devious monster with no discernible morals, and she had to remember that constantly.

The thick lashes of his heavy eyelids threw a shadow across his high cheekbones and she longed to touch his face, trace the contours.

'You actually look rather sexy in specs,' he said, calmly removing her glasses. At least, he sounded calm, yet she could feel the faint tremor in his fingertips as they brushed her skin. 'But I object to seeing all that glorious hair confined.'

'You can't do that.' It came out very shakily, and she wasn't at all surprised when he smiled and confidently began pulling out hairpins and lining them up on the desk.

Do something, Georgina! she screamed at herself furi-

ously. The pliancy pervading her was the most severe form
of bondage ever devised; few things could feel more addictive than the muscled barriers of his thighs. She struggled futilely against the delicious sensations aroused by
his fingers faintly touching her neck.

'I'm sure we can have a mutually beneficial arrangement
whilst our professional paths are entwined,' he mused as
he watched several gleaming strands slip over her shoulder.

The pragmatic words were like a slap in the face and
with a startled gasp of horror she pulled away, the slum-
brous expression dying from her eyes. 'Briefly entwined,'
she spat out, and relief flooded through her. The voice that
had emerged from her lips was confident and strong, not
that of a quivering wreck at all. After everything that had
happened she'd still been about to   Her mind shut off the
pathway she'd been skipping along seconds earlier; some
things didn't bear thinking about!

'You are going to safeguard your investment, then,' he
said, slowly getting to his feet. Apart from a brief flicker
of rage that vanished almost the same instant she imagined
she saw it, his equilibrium seemed untouched by her re-
covery.

Let him think what he liked; anything she was about to
do was for Oliver and the company that he had loved like
the son he'd never had, not for the money that Callum
imagined he could buy her with. More fool him! she
thought scornfully.

'I'll work my notice, certainly.'

'I thought you might.' The dryness made her wince.

'It must be comforting to be omnipotent,' she observed.
'Let me make it quite plain that whilst I work *with* you—'
she deliberately emphasised the word '—I won't tolerate
any sexual harassment.' The flicker of icy blue contempt
in his eyes made her cheeks grow hot. 'The only way you

got into my bed once was by pretending to be what you weren't. I thought you were a nice, harmless hunk and I needed comfort. Now I know you are a malicious, devious, unscrupulous rodent, and I'm never going to be *that* vulnerable!'

'I'm aware you're the sort of female incapable of sustaining an emotional relationship; it could be we have that much in common,' he observed wryly. 'Perhaps that's why you make me so mad. I see all the things in you I despise most about myself. However, under the circumstances it seems a waste of resources not to explore the mutual hunger we seem to have ignited.'

'Smoulder' had only been a word until she'd seen his eyes, she thought, riveted by the expression in the restless blue gaze. A black hole had replaced the pit of her belly and she was tempted to let the warm sensations writhing there envelop her. 'Despise about yourself?' She made a scornful sound. 'Strange. I had the impression you were rather pleased with yourself; you ooze self-satisfaction from every pore.'

She took a step backwards as she read retribution in the glitter in his eyes. One step further away and a myopic fog blurred the alarming vision. 'If you want to keep me sweet, Mr Stewart, you'd better be nice. I don't mean *that* nice,' she added hastily as she anticipated the gleam in his eyes. 'I'll tell you all I know about Oliver's deals and soothe worried clients; in return I want you to keep your distance.'

Surprisingly he gave a shrug. 'It might be best that way, but you'd do well to remember that ours is a relationship of mutual convenience.' The spurt of irrational pique that coursed through her made her chew on her lower lip as she struggled to keep her expression blank. 'I want to get away from Britain as soon as possible,' he said consideringly. 'Distractions would probably just hold things up.'

'You're going back to Australia?'

'Not immediately. I've acquired a property in France—the Languedoc, to be more accurate.'

'To farm?' she said, her eyes widening with surprise. I know nothing about him, she realised. He might even be married! The thought made her go cold with horror.

'My brother is the farmer, or grazier, as we term it back home. I make wine, Georgina.'

'You do?' She knew about as much about the popular Australian wines that were flooding the home market as anyone else of her acquaintance, which wasn't a lot. 'You're going to France to learn their techniques?'

He walked past her to the door, his demeanour dismissive enough to make her stiffen.

'I'm going to teach them *our* techniques,' he corrected her. 'Introducing new grape varieties and combining them will produce top-class products.' Despite his grim air she sensed the enthusiasm in his voice.

'I'm sure they'll be suitably appreciative,' she remarked, sweeping past him as he held open the door.

She ignored Mary's look of startled enquiry and was about to leave the small outer office when Callum appeared once more. 'I believe this is yours,' he observed, holding out the manila envelope. 'And these.' The hairgrips were dropped into her upturned palm. He proceeded to slide her spectacles back onto her nose. His features slid into focus as she blinked.

The bubble of righteous indignation into which she had crawled burst the instant she felt the blind force of primal attraction claw its way into her body. For an instant she froze under the impact of this brutal assault of her senses. To make matters worse she saw the flare of understanding in the eyes—understanding with no accompanying warmth; it was almost clinical and certainly calculating. Having her weakness recognised was the final humiliation!

She made some inarticulate sound and fled, aware of

what Mary must be thinking of her hair streaming down her back. If executives were prepared to turn cartwheels for him, what must she think mere PAs were willing to do? Georgina, you've already done it, she told herself, a bubble of hysteria rising in her throat. And look what it's landed you in. She hardly noticed the odd looks that followed her precipitate flight along the densely carpeted corridors.

CHAPTER SIX

'WORKING BREAKFAST' was the way the memo had termed it, but so far Georgina hadn't eaten anything. She replaced her coffee-cup on its saucer very carefully as she calmed herself to reply to the aggressive question of Simon May, the most logical successor to Oliver's position.

He was good-looking, in a florid sort of way, and until she'd seen him in the same room as Callum he'd seemed the epitome of cool self-assurance. Now his desire to score points had made him utter several snide and childish comments that had earned him a calculating appraisal from the man in charge.

She had been set to fend off Callum's disparaging remarks but it was Simon's attitude throughout the meeting that was patronising to the point of being overtly offensive.

'I'm sorry you find the overall campaign too simplistic, but it was what Oliver intended to deliver,' she said earnestly, trying not to react defensively. The client they were discussing was an airline which was one of Mallory's major customers.

'So you say.' This time he didn't bother to disguise his disdain.

'You are calling Miss Campion a liar?' The question was casually voiced. Of the eight people present Callum had said the least. The few comments he'd made had been searching and acute; he might know little about advertising but he obviously had an astute brain and he managed to cut through woolly statements and reveal the flaws with insulting ease. He had certainly been listening—critically, she was sure—to the way she was handling the resentful questions from the senior men present.

'I'm saying that basing our strategy on the say-so of a jumped-up clerk would be suicidal. We only have her word that Oliver intended any of this.'

'What reason would she have for lying?' Callum asked, his glance flicking to her taut profile. She was aware of the scrutiny and he knew she was, but her expression didn't flinch. He couldn't help but admire the sort of control she was displaying.

'And, perhaps more importantly, what alternative do you have in mind?' His voice was soft, but had an edge of authority that made the other man's eye contact waver. 'You and the gentlemen here represent approximately forty-three per cent of the company's accounts. Oliver was personally responsible for the remainder; how do you intend to persuade that fifty-plus per cent not to defect? None of you earned my uncle's confidence. Why should I give you mine?'

The calm presentation of the facts made Simon May's colour fluctuate dramatically. 'If I might say so, with all respect, sir, you have no experience of this business. It's difficult for an outsider to see—'

'I can *see* you're allowing personal animosity and ambition to blind you to the most important problem at hand. Your first loyalty should be to the shareholders, who will be the first to suffer if this agency is torn apart by internal wrangling. Take it from me, Simon, that Miss Campion has every reason to do her utmost to ensure this firm remains a strong, viable enterprise.'

He smiled thinly, his voice sandpaper-dry, and met her apprehensive glare momentarily before his attention shifted once more to the men present.

Georgina watched with a jumble of conflicting emotions

as Callum effortlessly dominated the proceedings. Would he be vindictive enough to reveal the legacy to them? If he did she knew there would be no possibility of her creating any sort of working relationship with the other senior executives.

'You will all acquaint yourselves with the details Miss Campion is able to provide. Contact with clients will be initiated by her as she is familiar with them.'

'She's just a...' Simon May's rather protuberant eyes looked about to leave their sockets and Georgina felt a surge of uncharitable glee. Still, she thought gloomily, he'd have the last laugh when he realised he'd already got his wish—because she was out of Mallory's. She knew none of this was in any way a personal campaign to defend her, but it felt strange hearing her cause being espoused by Callum of all people. Simon would be delighted if he knew that the new boss despised her even more than he did, she thought cynically.

She'd dealt with Simon's amorous campaign clumsily, she thought as she intercepted his malevolent, accusing glare. There had been witnesses when she had given him an acerbic put-down and every snigger he had suffered afterwards had been another nail in her coffin as far as he was concerned. She really ought to have made allowances for the fragility of the male ego, she decided wryly.

'Are you going to enlighten us as to what Miss Campion is?' Callum enquired with a lift of his eyebrows.

'She has been deliberately obstructive in the past,' Simon blustered after a brief, taut silence. 'It takes an account manager to understand the intricacies at this level—teamwork. She's never been part of any team.' Several people nodded their agreement. Though their working backgrounds were dissimilar they all had an impressive academic education to fall back on—one she couldn't match. To do their job required a mixture of artistic inspiration, commercial proficiency and the edge required to stay at the top in a highly competitive field.

She stifled a surge of uncertainty. Oliver believed in me, she told herself firmly. She refused to be made to appear inadequate in front of Callum. It was no concern of hers if he considered her morals to be non-existent, but she was damned if she was going to let him think she was incompetent.

'If you'd like to speak to the TV production people, I know that Oliver approached them informally concerning the campaign. They can confirm the bare bones of what I'm telling you.'

Georgina wasn't about to let any one of them intimidate her; she knew she was capable of doing the job Oliver had trained her for. Intuitively she knew that Callum would have admired Simon more if he'd favoured the more forthright approach rather than skirting around the issue. She knew to her cost that he wasn't tentative about voicing his own opinions!

'Oliver wasn't a team player either,' Callum interjected, much to her surprise.

'You can hardly equate a typist in a short skirt with Oliver Mallory,' Simon complained derisively.

'I'll make a note not to permit Miss Campion to wear distracting short skirts,' Callum said cryptically. 'As they bother you so much.' The frown which drew his dark brows together indicated that he was impatient with these petty comments. 'If she's obstructive, Simon, tell me.' His tone suggested a closure of the subject.

Georgina kept her head proudly erect and sent him a glare that told him exactly what he could do with his discipline. He might think she cared about her inheritance but the only reason why she cared about what any of them did was that she wanted to ensure Oliver's company wasn't killed off by rumour and speculation now that its guiding hand had gone.

'As to my lack of experience, gentlemen, whilst I don't consider that necessarily an impediment I have no wish to take control of the day-to-day running of the firm, although, for the present, I do intend to remain a major shareholder.'

They watched him with avid eyes, pretending various degrees of nonchalance with varied success. Although she didn't much care if Callum Stewart walked off the edge of the world Georgina found herself waiting with parted lips for the next instalment of his announcement.

'I expect you're all familiar with the name Peter Llewellyn.' Nobody disputed this. Peter Llewellyn was the managing director of one of the biggest New York advertising firms. 'He's accepted an offer to take over the reins here, as of next month.'

He stood up and gave them all a faint smile. 'I'll leave you to talk amongst yourselves. Georgina, I'll speak with you...' Blue eyes flicked over her, moving upwards from her neatly crossed ankles to her smooth, gleaming head. 'Now...please.' The latter was added as a definite afterthought. He strode from the room without a backward glance, taking her compliance as read.

She got to her feet with as much dignity as possible. The animosity around the table had been difficult enough to cope with without her very special problems in dealing with Callum Stewart. Simon May also rose and effectively blocked her way.

'It didn't take you long to slip between his sheets, did it, sweetheart?' he sneered. 'Still, I doubt if you'll find it quite so easy to lead him by the nose as the old man.'

'You really are a bad loser, Simon.' She injected a shade of amusement into her voice and pitched it loud enough to be heard throughout the room. 'Just because you're prepared to sell your soul for promotion you assume everyone else is for sale too. Shame all that boot-licking went to waste.'

Several faces watched Simon with no sign of sympathy. His aspirations were no secret and his style had won him few friends amongst his peers. Being passed over for the top job was bad enough, but Callum's attitude had made it pretty clear to everyone present that he hadn't even been in the running.

'Bitch,' he muttered as she swept past.

She went to the washroom to rinse her face with cold water before presenting herself. It took her a few minutes to do some lightning repairs to her make-up. Mary's eyes were fixed on the door as she entered the outer office and Georgina knew the woman had been waiting for her arrival.

'He's waiting for you,' she said, indicating the ajar door.

'I'm quivering with anticipation,' Georgina snapped, and immediately felt guilty at the tone she'd used with her friend. But before she could apologise another voice distracted her.

'That's gratifying to hear.' The door swung wider on its hinges to reveal Callum.

'Eavesdropping is a disgusting habit,' she observed as she went into his office, and almost giggled as she heard Mary's audible hiss of dismay. I'm already sacked; at least, I would be if I hadn't resigned first, she mentally corrected herself. He can't do much worse, she decided without too much confidence.

'Do have a seat.'

'I prefer to stand.'

'You handled yourself rather well back there.'

This unexpected endorsement made her blink. 'That surprised you,' she observed drily. Because I'm an incompetent who earns her salary by flattering old men and

worse, she thought bitterly. She ignored her initial gratification at his words and concentrated grimly on her anger.

'As does the fact you've been crying.' He spoke as if
he was angry that she'd displayed this feminine weakness.
'What did Simon say after I'd gone?' He moved with fascinating animal grace to the other side of the room. Just
watching him made the muscles deep in her belly spas-
modically tighten. Her throat felt constricted as he turned
from her and looked out across the city.

'I haven't been crying,' she responded swiftly—too
swiftly, she realised, biting her lip.

He turned his head slightly, his expression reflecting his
impatient disbelief. 'Is there something personal between
you two?' he asked bluntly.

She gave an instinctive grimace of fastidious distaste.
'Certainly not,' she retorted crisply. 'Not that it'd be anything to do with you if there were,' she added as an afterthought.

'Why the look of outrage?' he asked, moving away from
the window. He thrust his hands deep into the pockets of
his trousers and watched her with a brooding expression
that made her wonder just what thoughts were forming
behind those brilliantly blue eyes. 'After all, you do have
a peculiarly strong effect on men and are not averse to
using it to your own advantage. Was Simon a stepping-
stone to your real objective? If so, I can understand his
bitterness. As for it being my business, anything that in-
terferes with the smooth running of this agency is exactly
that.'

'Has it never occurred to you I might be just plain good
at what I do?' Arms akimbo, she flung the words at him.
'The men around here just feel threatened at having their
male territory invaded. If I'd been a man who'd leap-
frogged a few steps up the ladder I'd be a real go-getter,
a whizkid, but because I'm a woman I'm trading on my

sexuality. You didn't know your uncle very well if you think he'd tolerate fools, no matter how good their legs were.'

Throat suddenly dry, she paused for breath. 'Not that mine are, but…' The afterthought came as she saw the direction his gaze had taken. Taking into account the fact that she had few secrets—at least physically—left from him, her acute embarrassment was absurd, she knew.

'I find it strange that you're prepared to sell your abilities so aggressively and yet appear modest about your physical attributes,' he said, openly sceptical. The husky, uneven quality to his voice made her quiver. This reluctant fascination with every minor detail about him made every second in his company a balancing act of maintaining her dignity. 'I think under the circumstances you can drop the *ingénue* acts in front of me. I know you're a sensual woman with very grown-up appetites.'

'How did you manage to persuade Peter Llewellyn to come here at such short notice?' she asked, rubbing her clammy hands against the dark fabric of her skirt. The less she thought about her appetites the better!

Callum's wry expression acknowledged her unsubtle change of subject. 'We've been friends since we were at Harvard Business School together. I know I'm meant to be wet behind the ears so don't spread the news I'm not straight from the bush; it's useful to be underestimated occasionally.' There was a glimmer of humour in his blue eyes. 'Peter's tired of being a big cog in someone else's machine. He's been on the lookout for a fresh challenge for some time. I've given him the option to buy out my share in three years' time if things work out.'

'Why are you telling *me* this?' she asked frankly.

'I thought your discretion was legendary?' he said mockingly.

She looked at him in open confusion. 'You don't trust me,' she protested.

'On a personal level, never,' he agreed. Why she should feel so devastated by this piece of blunt honesty was mystifying. 'Professionally I might have to consider,' he conceded. 'So long as I keep in mind you're a hungry lady, and I use the term loosely, striving hard to get to the top.'

'Big of you,' she observed, her voice tinged with anger.

'I think so,' he agreed benignly. 'I don't like ambitious women, but I can appreciate talent. Did Oliver use you to deliberately needle the designer suits out there?' he asked, settling into the big chair and committing the sacrilege of putting his feet up onto the gleaming mahogany of the vast desk. He loosened his tie as he turned the full glare of his scrutiny onto her.

The swift shift from formality to this relaxed style had her brain working overtime to see what hidden agenda was behind the false sense of security his attitude was creating. Also, his propensity for seeing the hidden motive was uncanny; anyone would think the devil could read minds!

'He liked to keep them on their toes,' she admitted reluctantly. 'Also, he could be genuinely paranoid about confidentiality, as you must have guessed. He didn't want anyone else muscling in on his clients; he liked to be the one they wanted. But then I suppose we all like to be indispensable to someone.' She gave a faint, bitter smile. 'I think he was quite flattered when people thought I was…' She paused, hot colour seeping beneath the creamy tinge of her skin as she realised she'd voiced her private speculations out loud.

'You mean you managed to keep him dangling on a string. How clever of you.'

'I'm not responsible for the sordid state of people's minds,' she snapped.

'If they knew about your little windfall I'm sure even the most charitable would imagine the worst.'

As he did, of course, she thought bitterly. 'Is that a threat?' she asked derisively. 'I didn't ask your uncle for anything except a chance to show what I could do. I haven't the faintest idea why he made such a gesture.' Though, knowing Oliver, there had to be some reason; he had never done anything without a reason. Her troubled mind returned to the unopened manila envelope. She still hadn't been able to bring herself to examine its contents.

'I don't know why you don't come clean with me, Georgina. I'm not interested in your morals, just the smooth running of this firm.'

'That's rich,' she said incredulously. 'It seems to me you're exceedingly interested in my morals. Just because I spent one night with you you seem to think you're the world authority on me. Why am I classed as the tramp? Weren't you there that night too?'

The air of casual humour dissipated in the blink of an eye. His legs shot down from their resting place and he was on his feet in an instant.

'*I* was also there in the morning. Which reminds me, I have something that belongs to you.' He withdrew a handful of notes from his wallet and flung them at her. Caught in a warm current of air, the pieces of paper fluttered slowly to the floor. 'I'm not liberated enough to allow a woman to pay for my room.'

She ignored the action, telling herself such childishness was beneath her contempt, but she couldn't ignore the lick of pure rage that was visible in his eyes.

'I made a mistake,' she said flatly. 'Even before I realised who you were.' She almost choked on her sense of outrage. What right did he have to act so superior? Anyone would think he was the injured party. 'Do you think I would have slept with you if I'd known the truth?' she demanded, her voice hoarse with anger. 'You knew that. Why else would you have carried on with the subterfuge?'

'You're the one who wanted me to act a part. How was I to know how far you wanted it go to?' he bit back. 'Or have you chosen to forget that you instigated one deception? It just gave birth to another. As for telling you who I was, at the moment you're talking about we were both fairly incapable of thinking much past the gratification of our primitive needs.' His glittering gaze challenged her to deny this version of affairs.

But Georgina was far too concerned with coping with the surge of life that jolted her composure to its foundations. Images spun in her head to torment and tease her; even closing her eyes didn't block them. When she opened them again he continued, his tone now caustic and harsh.

'You took away any opportunity for me to remedy the situation when you sneaked away like a thief in the night.'

Thief? If anyone had had anything stolen it was her! But innate honesty made her bite back this retort. He hadn't taken anything she hadn't been anxious to give away. The awful irony of it was that, even now, in the midst of hating him, she could still see how easy it would be to give again. It was difficult to think straight when she was reliving those intimate moments.

'Am I supposed to believe you'd have done that?' she sneered with as much scorn as she could muster. The fact that even the humiliating truth couldn't kill off this attraction she felt towards him was difficult to cope with. 'Or were you just looking forward to seeing me squirm, having totally humiliated me?'

Contempt darkened his eyes as he held her gaze. 'I did nothing to you you didn't want. If you choose to call it humiliation, that's up to you.'

He gave a shrug and slid his tie back into place. His slipped control also seemed firmly back in place, and despite the subject matter his attitude was that of someone speaking to an employee—which was all she was, she reminded herself firmly.

'I'm not taking full responsibility for the situation, if that's what you're after. I was in the right place at the right time. The female of the species like to act as though lust is something only men are afflicted with, but we both know different, Georgina.'

The scorn in her laugh made his lips tighten. Despite the air-conditioning her clothes stuck to her skin as cold perspiration broke out over her body; the effort required to stay in the room was physical. Her thoughts were in turmoil; his jibe had made her examine something that had been sitting on the edge of her consciousness. The sense of empathic recognition she'd felt when she'd first seen him—it had gone deeper than merely physical for her, no matter what he said.

No other man had ever been able to break down the protective barriers she'd constructed. What she'd felt for Alex had been negligible when she recalled the state of chaos she'd been in since she'd met this man. How often had Alex even crossed her mind these last days? The guilty answer made her wince.

'I think you already know you were a substitute,' she said, and from somewhere she summoned a gentle mocking smile. Inside, her heart was being constricted by an iron hand.

After a pulse of pure fury, which, given her words, couldn't be wondered at, ice descended over his expression. 'I won't keep you.' He glanced pointedly at his wristwatch. 'I'm expecting someone. I want to know how you get on today; I'll meet you for dinner.'

The dismissal and the cool order made her bristle with antagonism. Dinner and Callum was a combination she knew she should avoid at all costs, even had the invitation been made in an acceptable manner. If he thought he could click his fingers and she'd come running it was about time she taught him that this was not the case.

'I don't want to go to dinner with you.'

'Then you can watch me eat,' he said, eyeing her in a bored fashion that only intensified her indignation. 'I have a heavy schedule; tonight is the only time I can see you and I have no intention of fasting for your benefit. You look like a woman who likes her food.'

Her bosom swelled in anger as his eyes slid over her gentle curves. 'Are you implying I'm fat?' The second the words were out of her mouth she wished she could snatch them back. The pettish comment only invited personal observations likely to shrivel her with mortification.

His eyelids lowered over the brilliant glare of his eyes but she knew they were moving over her body and the tension in the room suddenly seemed stretched tight enough to snap. 'I'd say your flesh-to-bone ratio is as near perfect as it gets,' he said drily.

The oddly impersonal compliment gave her a small spurt of irrational dissatisfaction. 'I'm not a horse,' she snapped.

The concealing fringe of eyelashes lifted and her breath caught as she saw that his glance was anything but impersonal. 'I'm painfully aware of that, but I thought you might not care for a more comprehensive appreciation of your physical attributes in the office environment. I wouldn't like to be accused of sexual harassment,' he said mockingly. 'But if you're interested...I could tell you how incredibly sensuous I find the way your hips flare out from your waist and the dimple you have—'

'No, don't!' Repelled by and conversely drawn to the words that slid like honey from his lips, she backed away, reaching for and eventually finding the doorhandle.

Callum's lips quirked in a wry smile that indicated he

understood the ambiguity of her feelings. Not all of the heat died from his sombre eyes. 'I'll expect an update this evening, then. Be ready at eight.'

She was so anxious to escape the confines of the room that she didn't even feel angry at the peremptory order. Just out of the door, she almost collided with a tall brunette. She pushed her spectacles further up the bridge of her nose and mumbled an apology.

She received a glowing smile in return and a cheerful, 'No problem.' The girl's attention slid away from her and Georgina turned her head in time to see her fling herself with unselfconscious enthusiasm into Callum's open arms. 'Cal, angel, I've got the most brilliant news.'

Georgina heard him laugh; it was such an uncomplicated sound of pure pleasure, echoing the expression on his face, that it hurt. She turned away, conscious only of the pain that throbbed in her temples and the slick churning in her stomach. She walked past Mary, aware that, to her, every time she emerged from Callum's office she must look like a candidate for resuscitation. Come to think of it, she *felt* like a candidate for resuscitation!

Consciously she straightened her shoulders, and her chin went up as she assumed a cheerful expression. 'Who was that, Mary?' she asked casually.

'Tricia Stewart,' Mary replied, and the sympathy in her eyes made Georgina shift uncomfortably. 'Mrs Stewart,' she added in a small, apologetic tone.

'I see,' Georgina said carefully. Why should I care if he's married to *thirty* women? she asked herself. I would never knowingly have slept with a married man. The mixture of envy, guilt and sympathy she experienced as she thought of that glowing girl was suffocating. Rage licked along her veins; he had placed her in an impossible position! He was a faithless pig. Wait until tonight! She'd have a few home truths to deliver to Mr Callum Stewart. She placed her fingers to her throbbing temples. God, he might even have children!

To work off her fury she concentrated with grim tenacity on her work and made a gratifying amount of headway. Ironically, the faster she achieved her goals, the nearer she got to making herself redundant as far as Mallory's was concerned. Still, the sooner she was in a position never to see Callum again the better!

'You're not dressed.'

The words shattered the instant of *déjà vu* as she opened the door to the tall, rugged stranger. Only now he wasn't a stranger...anything but. He looked distressingly drop-dead gorgeous in the dark formal suit and she compressed her lips, hating her intense appreciation of the fact and wishing her nose weren't sensitive to the elusive fragrance that drifted from his body.

'I am dressed,' she contradicted him firmly. She glanced down at her jeans which had seen better days and the pale blue shirt knotted loosely at her waist.

He made an impatient sound in his throat and pushed past her. She closed the door. Short of calling for armed assistance, she decided philosophically, she had no way of evicting him forcibly. 'Make yourself at home,' she said sarcastically, following him into the sitting room.

'You've got ten minutes to get ready.'

'You may be able to order me around like some sort of tinpot dictator at the office, but I'm not paid to suffer you out of office hours,' she observed flatly, folding her arms across her chest. The action caused her shirt to rise up, revealing a portion of her smooth, flat midriff, and she hastily lowered her arms to her side. His glance had homed in on the expanse of flesh and she saw, rather to her surprise, colour suffuse the crest of his cheekbones.

'I'm a firm believer in flexi-hours,' he said with a husky

rasp in his voice. 'Get dressed, Georgina; I'm hungry.' The expression she glimpsed in his eyes made his words open to interpretation and her knees turn to cotton wool. 'If you don't get dressed I'll help you.'

'You wouldn't dare!' A quirk of one well-defined eyebrow and a slow smile dispelled any illusions she had on that score. 'I don't want to go to dinner with you.' A sudden sound emerged from between her clenched teeth. Half-anguish, half-outrage. 'What about your wife?' God, I was going to taunt him with a nice mixture of composure and disdain and here I am squeaking like an agitated mouse, she thought.

The deep blue eyes which had been narrowed in speculation suddenly widened. The rat! she thought wrathfully. He only feels guilty when he's caught out. 'Which one would that be?' he enquired with cautious interest.

'Very droll,' she snapped. 'Though I doubt if Tricia would appreciate the humour. Being made party to adultery is not my idea of a joke either.'

'Actually I've arranged to meet her for drinks after dinner. You can come along too as you're so interested in my personal life.' His smile grew as her bosom heaved in agitation.

'She knows about us?'

'Us.' He gave a soulful sigh. 'You do care after all. What's wrong, Georgina?' he asked with a perplexed look. 'Do you have a problem with the arrangement?'

'Why, you...' Colour wildly fluctuating, she stared at him in sick horror.

'She'll be with her husband—my brother—if that makes a difference.'

Sister-in-law! She felt her cheeks ignite with fiery embarrassment. 'Oh,' she said in a rather forlorn voice.

He folded his arms across his chest and she could see the shadow of body hair through the thin fabric of his shirt.

Her stomach muscles quivered as she tried hard to avert her stare. 'You weren't so tongue-tied a few minutes ago when reading me the Riot Act. Is that all the apology I'm going to get?'

'Under the circumstances it was a perfectly natural mistake to make,' she said defensively. Apologising to him was marginally more difficult than chopping off her own finger.

'Which circumstances are those? Your lurid imagination, or your high opinion of my moral fibre?'

She sniffed. 'I should have known no woman would be fool enough to marry you.'

'I didn't say I wasn't married,' he interjected softly.

She swallowed hard. 'Well…are you?' she said tightly as he continued to watch her with that infuriating sphinx-like impassivity. 'It's bad enough I slept with you at all without that.'

A curious expression entered his eyes. 'It would bother you that much?'

'As a matter of fact, yes, it would.'

'From that am I to infer you believe in the sanctity of marriage and all that jazz?' His tone was faintly mocking but his eyes, holding hers, were strangely serious. 'I think you'll find scruples like that might hinder your meteoric rise, Georgina.'

'You still haven't answered me.' He really did like to extract every last ounce of agony from a situation, she thought resentfully.

He reached forward and his thumb stroked across the side of her cheek. 'Always the best man, never the groom,' he said sorrowfully.

'Best!' She snorted, flinching away from the touch which prickled like an electrical current across her skin. 'That's a matter of opinion,' she said huskily. The anxiety dissolved, only to be replaced by another tension, one no less intense.

'I'm surprised your cynical little heart has room for such elevated moral standards, let alone any belief in the sanctity of marriage. I thought the scars of your parents' marriage would have cured you of any romantic notions.'

What had she told him? She flushed, recalling the disastrous wedding day when her unguarded confidences had spilled out. Of late she'd had reason to question her judgemental attitude towards her mother's weaknesses. Having experienced firsthand how powerful the blind, primitive force to mate could be, her smug, complacent superiority had been shaken to its core.

'I know men are congenitally incapable of being faithful.'

'Isn't that a bit sweeping?'

'I think my illusions are my concern, not yours, but be assured I have none about you.'

'Actually we're both the product of unsuccessful marriages,' he observed with a thin smile. 'Dysfunctional—isn't that the popular term? I'm surprised you were so anxious to perpetuate the error yourself, but then history does suggest people are incapable of learning by their mistakes. Or, in this case, your parents' mistakes.'

'Don't you intend to marry?' she asked curiously.

'Not to satisfy any primitive desire to possess a woman. That situation can be achieved without any formal contract,' he said, his eyes flicking over her with insulting familiarity. 'Choosing a mate shouldn't be done in a rush of hormones or for mushily sentimental reasons,' he said with confident scorn. 'I shall marry someone whose expectations are similar to my own.'

Does such a creature exist? she wondered doubtfully. She was glad her own experiences hadn't left her quite that disillusioned. What had soured Callum Stewart so profoundly? 'Will you have children? Or will that be too messy?' she asked sarcastically. She was appalled by the sterile scenario he painted of marriage. Could a man who was obviously capable of passion really be satisfied with such an arrangement?

'That's the only reason I'd ever consider entering into that particular contract.'

'I hope the job pays well,' she observed flippantly. 'Because you might find there aren't too many takers.'

'Thanks for the concern, but I wasn't considering you for the post.'

'I'm devastated,' she hissed.

'I know I'm a fascinating subject but aren't you going to get dressed?'

Georgina gave a sigh of pure frustration. 'I can give you a progress report here,' she said. 'Though why the morning won't do…'

'In the morning I'm off to France,' he explained shortly. With an expression she didn't trust he looked thoughtfully around the room, his eyes dwelling outrageously on the open door to her bedroom. 'Mind you, an evening in might be quite cosy,' he observed silkily. 'Can you cook?' he enquired, all blue-eyed innocence.

His husky laughter followed her retreat to the bedroom and, leaning against the door, she gave a tremulous sigh. He'd been baiting her, she knew it, but if he'd known how beguiling the idea had been—cooking for Callum, sharing the food and her small, narrow bed…

I'm going mad! She licked her dry lips and raked a hand through her hair with a trembling hand. Seeing him in public was a far safer bet than seeing him in privacy, she decided, opening her wardrobe door and surveying the contents with a frown.

She hadn't selected her outfit with any desire to please him, she told herself firmly, surveying the end product of her deliberations a few minutes later. This dress was the one she always wheeled out on vaguely dressy occasions. It was the archetypal little black number—a plain sleeveless shift with a row of beading around the above-the-knee-length hemline that made the garment move against her legs as she walked with a pleasing swishing sensation that had always seemed deliciously decadent to her.

Decadent was not a frame of mind she ought to cultivate at this particular moment! she thought, her second attempt to pin up her hair ending in another failure as a shower of clips slid down her neck and the heavy tresses followed suit, spilling down her back like a river touched with the lustre of a setting sun. She stifled a sound of frustration.

'If you're not ready in thirty seconds I'll come and help.'

The voice from the other room made her throw down her hairbrush and, after a brief glance at her freshly applied lipstick, head for the door. I never was much good at entrances, she thought wryly, pausing with her hand on the doorhandle, but here goes!

She decided to look everywhere but at Callum, which was quite difficult because it wasn't a big room and he was a big man. He certainly seemed to make things seem distinctly claustrophobic.

'I know a lot of women—'

'I just bet you do,' she snapped.

'—who would envy you for being able to produce this sort of result in minutes.'

She blinked, swallowed convulsively and forgot she wasn't going to look into those eyes—eyes that seemed deep enough to drown in. God, I'm getting positively mushy, she thought with vaguely desperate humour. The black rings around his irises made the colour appear even more dense. It was the expression in them, not the colour, however, that made her twitch the hem of her dress like a nervous child.

A muscle flexed along his angular jaw as he contemplated the picture she made standing watching him with wide-eyed trepidation. The sensuous appreciation of his expression shifted to something else before abruptly hardening. He straightened up and made a sharp gesture towards the door. 'Time we were off.'

Close but not touching, he ushered her down to his car.

'More room in this than my Beetle for your legs,' she observed, sinking into the leather upholstery. It was a long, low-slung coupé—the sort of thing which made people stare, which was a definite detraction from its obvious attractions in her mind. She wished quite a lot that she hadn't thought about his legs—long, athletic legs with just the right amount of muscle power and that light sprinkling of dark hair.

Callum slid in beside her but he didn't appear to notice her comment. Her furtive glance in the direction of his legs and her visible gulp he did notice. 'I like your legs too,' he said in a low, throaty voice that made all the small, downy hairs on her arms stand on end.

She gave a startled gasp and turned her head to look at him. It was like stepping off a cliff; the warm, dark chasm was frightening yet heart-stoppingly enticing. He reached out a hand and traced the line of her collar-bone. It moved to the angle of her chin and cradled her jaw. She found her cheek turning to rest in the large palm.

'We don't have to go to dinner,' he suggested, and the smoky invitation in his voice liquefied every ounce of her resistance. Molten and warm, the desire moved through her pliant body like a storm.

In a minute he was going to kiss her and the anticipation was unbearable. She could hear the harsh sound of her swift inhalations as her whole body centred on the immi-

nent invasion of his mouth…the taste and texture. The
blast of a horn and the glaring lights of a passing car were
all that stopped the escalation of this insanity.

She drew back, placing her hands on her lips. 'For
God's sake, start the car up!' she pleaded, not looking at
him.

He cursed with impressive fluency and the car shot forward. Georgina was learning fast not to overestimate her
own powers of resistance or his of perseverance. It was a
humbling lesson.

CHAPTER SEVEN

'THEY APPEAR TO know you here,' Georgina observed, after Callum had ordered the wine without consulting her. At least he hadn't interrupted as she'd given her order; she ought to be grateful that at least his appalling take-charge style didn't extend that far. She glanced at her starter and smiled faintly at the waiter, who silently withdrew.

'I'm staying here.'

The knowledge that he had a room just a lift-ride away made her neck ache even more than it already did; her muscles were twisted in tortured knots of tension. Heat scalded the back of her eyes as she briefly let her mind run over a scenario where Callum led her back to his room. The graphic images didn't end there! With a horrified start she halted her wayward imagination.

'You can drink it,' he said, nodding at her untouched wine. 'I'm not trying to get you drunk. You fall asleep, I seem to remember.'

Recalled from her abstraction, she gave him a glare of dislike. 'You really enjoy reminding me of that, don't you?' Self-disgust shone in her eyes as she looked at him.

'Are you always so tough on yourself?'

'I'll leave that to you,' she responded, surprised by his question.

'I won't make any allowances for you just because of our personal relationship,' he conceded.

'We don't *have* a relationship,' she retorted, twisting her napkin in her lap, her fingers trembling slightly.

'Has it thrown your calculations, actually wanting to sleep with me?'

She glared at his superbly confident features with simmering resentment. 'You really do think you're irresistible, don't you?' she breathed incredulously. 'It borders on the pathetic,' she added scornfully.

'At least you made...what was he called?...Alex jealous. Wasn't that what you set out to do?' Callum asked with the sort of smug superiority that made her teeth clamp hard on her lower lip. 'If we're talking pathetic...'

'I wasn't prepared to pay that price.'

'You seemed to enjoy paying the price at the time,' he observed, with a reminiscent look that sent hot colour flooding into her cheeks. 'Don't take the moral high ground with me, Georgina; you're as susceptible to the same appetites as the rest of us.'

'I thought you wanted a report,' she snapped. The petulant sound in her voice made her wince.

'I'm listening,' he said shortly. Leaning back in his chair, he levelled his disconcerting, unblinking stare directly at her.

He did listen, interrupting only to ask a few pertinent questions. 'You've been a busy little bee, haven't you?' he said when she'd finished.

'Denigrating and patronising are two terms which immediately spring to mind,' she observed, stabbing her asparagus-flavoured mousse with unwarranted force. She speared a prawn and bit into it viciously. She'd not just done well, she'd achieved miracles, and pacified several ruffled male egos into the bargain.

Amazingly he laughed. 'I'm impressed. Is that better?' The cleft that bisected his square chin deepened as he grinned.

'Much better,' she agreed huskily. He did have the most extraordinarily attractive laugh, she thought with a hint of wistfulness. 'I thought you were hungry; you haven't touched anything.' Her eyes flicked to his plate, partly to force her gaze away from his face.

'If I had, you'd probably have accused me of not giving you my undivided attention,' he observed with a teasing note in his voice. 'You don't treat me with the deference I've grown to expect, Georgina,' he told her, self-mockery flavouring his words. 'I've never been called sir so frequently in my life as since I arrived here.'

'There's not much point in me joining the queue to lick your boots; I'm already sacked, aren't I?'

'You handed in your notice, as I recall,' he said drily.

'It amounts to the same thing. I just beat you to it, that's all. Or are you going to say you hadn't intended throwing me out on my ear?'

'When it came down to it I just couldn't bear to be parted from you, darling.' His blue-eyed mockery made her teeth clench. 'I was forgetting that now you're a woman of substance you can afford to behave recklessly. Can't you, Georgina?'

The cynical twist of his lips as much as his words spoilt the brief illusion of harmony. Behaving recklessly was what had created this hateful situation to begin with!

'It's marvellous,' she agreed. 'I don't even have to sleep with the boss any more. Such a relief,' she drawled, rolling her eyes heavenwards. She saw his lips curl in disdain.

'I thought you managed to keep Oliver at arm's length *and* hold his interest, or was that just an idle boast? You're such a very versatile girl, I was inclined to believe you. I'm your boss now...you could sleep with me,' he offered generously. 'But it won't get you mentioned in my will, or even promoted.'

She wasn't calm enough to decide whether he really did think she was an unscrupulous slut or just enjoyed insulting her, but she wanted, quite desperately, to wipe that supercilious smirk off his face! 'In that case it's hardly worth my while, is it? I'll pass,' she said from between lips firmly committed to a smile. 'After all, isn't Peter Llewellyn going to be the man who matters in future? I'll practise my sultry seduction on him. Incidentally, I really admire you for admitting you're just not up to the task of running the agency.'

'I can't get worked up about the packaging of a new chocolate bar or the packaging of a recycled politician,' he agreed with a shrug. 'Call it a genetic flaw. Mallory's needs someone dynamic at the helm and no one in-house had the requirements. At least with Peter available I don't have to waste any more time here. Oliver knew I wouldn't be stepping into his shoes, but he also knew I wouldn't let what he'd built up crumble. He had no children; I think the agency was his contribution to posterity.'

'I think that's sad.'

'So do I,' he agreed unexpectedly.

She was still angry with him for the offhand, disparaging way he'd spoken about the agency. 'Of course, you're probably happier treading grapes or doing something rustic and fulfilling.' For some bizarre reason she suddenly had a vivid image of Callum stripped to the waist, his skin gleaming with labour's sweat, and she lost the thread of her vitriolic outburst completely. A small, inarticulate gurgle escaped her lips and she picked up her glass and took a healthy swallow of the pale liquid. Callum's own children would be conceived in a heartless marriage of convenience if he was to be believed.

'Do you like that?'

His words took her by surprise but she nodded as she tasted the warm, buttery aftertaste on her tongue and struggled to regain her composure.

'Then I must have been treading the grapes properly,' he said, watching her eyes dart to the bottle. 'A nice Chardonnay, but our Botrytis Semillon is the best thing we've done yet. It's an intense, late-harvest wine that I personally think can rival the best Sauternes available,' he observed confidently. 'New South Wales has a climate not dissimilar to that of the South of France. In Wollundra, for example, we're lucky with the climate; it's a hilly area and quite far south. I think you'll find our label on a lot of the better wine lists.

'As for the property... When it comes down to it, you're right—it is a farm, on a large scale. Doing what I do, I can be involved in every stage from the planting of the vines to the distribution and marketing. I find it satisfying to see the end result of my labour and to know the label—' he touched the striking gold motif on the bottle '—will be seen as a guarantee of quality.' His voice had a vibrant edge of enthusiasm and she realised how inspiring he could be when he chose to exercise his authority.

'Each to his own, I suppose,' she conceded. 'You have all that,' she said, 'yet you're off to France to start all over again. Some people are never satisfied.' In his own way Callum was as driven to succeed as Oliver had been, and, she suspected, just as ruthless.

'I like a challenge,' he said simply. 'Wollundra is in safe hands.'

'If you have a brother why didn't Oliver leave the company to you both? Your brother must be the elder.' She thought she might as well take advantage of his unusually expansive mood to satisfy some of her curiosity.

'Why do you say that?'

'He has the property, doesn't he? The elder-son-inheriting-the-kingdom thing.' Callum's words hadn't actually spelt it out but he obviously belonged to the Antipodean landed gentry.

'Rick is my younger brother. My half-brother,' he added, his expression strangely shuttered.

'Then why—?' she began.

'You really are a curious little cat, aren't you?' he observed, leaning over the table. His gaze touched the line of her throat, making a natural progression downwards until it reached the high curve of her bosom. His large, capable hands curled on the table and she watched his knuckles grow white.

An illicit excitement sent a surge of searing heat through her body. She imagined his hands stroking her skin and she had the curious conviction that his own imagination was running along similar lines.

'Oliver's sister—my mother—is Ruth Mallory.'

'The opera singer!' she said with a gasp of shock that jolted her free of the sensual preoccupation. For one thing Ruth Mallory didn't look old enough to be the parent of this specimen of manhood and, for another, Oliver had never mentioned a word about his sister's fame.

'Is there any other?' he drawled. 'Mother spent the first year of my life at Wollundra before she decided her interrupted career meant more to her than a husband and baby.'

His sneer held black humour, and exposure to his emotions made Georgina experience a paralysing surge of empathy. She swallowed hard to control the strength of her emotional response.

'My dad was devastated,' he continued sombrely. 'But, happily for him, he met Susie, Rick's mom, and the happy ending was in sight. When Dad remarried, my mother suddenly rediscovered maternal bonding and my presence at her side became essential for her continued happiness.' His cynical smile deepened and his eyes grew cold as he recalled the past. '*She* didn't want her "happy family," but Susie sure as hell wasn't going to have it.'

His eyes were expressionless as they flicked over her face but Georgina could feel the bitterness behind each word. 'After that I paid the odd flying visit to Wollundra when Ruth couldn't find anywhere else to dump me.' The resentment was under control and muted now, but Georgina could see that coming to terms with it had taken him time and effort.

'Rick grew up on the land; it's his.' He moved his hands in an expansive, elegant gesture. 'Dad wanted to—' He broke off and shook his head dismissively. Stupidly she wanted to brush back the wing of hair that flopped onto his forehead. 'I got what I wanted—the piece of land my grandmother had grown vines on when they'd pioneered the place. She was of Italian extraction...perhaps it's in the blood.' His grin was unselfconsciously charismatic. 'Life history over... Happy now?'

She had the impression he vaguely regretted telling her so much, enough to fire her imagination so she could fill in any blanks for herself. She could clearly see the boy, torn from the land and family he loved, used as an accessory for a glittering celebrity. Some people might have grown to envy and hate the half-brother who had, to all intents and purposes, taken their place, but Georgina only heard affection in Callum's voice when he spoke of the younger man. And his deep antipathy to her was easily explained now he equated what he viewed as her ruthless ambition with that of the famous diva.

'Your father must have known what your mother was when he married her,' she heard herself protesting.

'He was blinded by love,' Callum sneered disdainfully. 'Or at least a strong sexual attraction,' he moderated. 'Such a purely physical attraction couldn't be expected to withstand the realities of life. Like us, they should have had a wild fling and then just sent Christmas cards to each other,' he said, with a flippancy that cut her somewhere deep inside. 'It would have saved a lot of grief in the end.'

His sudden reference to their own situation made her knock over her wine. A waiter politely dismissed her stumbling apologies and she was glad the incident gave her time to gather her straying wits.

'Perhaps your parents weren't blessed with divine fore-sight, unlike you. Mind you, it's gone astray this time. I've no intention of having an affair, wild or otherwise, with you.'

His feral smile in response to her pugnacious announce-ment filled her with a deep sense of foreboding. 'Perhaps I didn't satisfy you in bed,' he suggested silkily.

Under the unremitting interrogation of his blue eyes she flushed uncomfortably. Was he too recalling her hoarse cries of astonishment and husky entreaty? It was devastat-ing to recall, at any time, the way her passion and need had escalated. Under the glittering glare of his eyes it was agonising.

'Do you want marks out of ten?'

He shifted in his seat and tugged unconsciously at the restricting silk tie around his neck. The warm colour seep-ing beneath his tan revealed that he was not as totally in control of himself as his attitude might imply. 'Do you want to carry on as though nothing has happened between us?'

'As far as I'm concerned, nothing—nothing of impor-tance, that is—has,' she said stubbornly.

'Is that a challenge?' he asked. With an air of quiet desperation she watched his long fingers holding the knife as her stomach tied itself in knots. 'Don't confuse impor-tance with urgency.'

'Urgency?' she croaked, feeling her hard-won compo-sure sliding away under the pressure of his voice.

'I'm just stating what we both know is fact,' he contin-ued inexorably.

'We're talking about a one-night stand here, Callum. Nice enough as that sort of thing goes, but not mind-blowing enough to make me lose sleep. I know this may come as a shock but there was nothing wrong with my life before you entered it!'

'Sure,' he sneered. 'You have such a fulfilling existence that you were reduced to hiring an escort to save your face. You must really have rubbed your boyfriend's nose in your infidelities to make him break it off. The guy was visibly drooling over you.'

'He was not!' she snapped. 'For your information Alex found me lacking in the bedroom department.' Georgina closed her eyes and inwardly groaned as the bitter little response slipped impetuously from her.

'Did he, now?' Callum let out a silent whistle from between his pursed lips. 'How informative.'

'Love and sex are not the same thing,' she said defensively, abandoning all pretence of doing justice to the meal before her.

'Maybe, but love sure as hell isn't that neat emotion you seem to think it is,' he responded scornfully. 'Did you fall in love with that guy because he had the right qualifications for the job? Did you believe him when he accused you of being frigid? It must have occurred to you that *he* might be doing something wrong.'

'You mean I should have referred him to my previous lovers?' she choked.

'Awkward,' he agreed. 'Couldn't you have faked it?'

'I do not fake it!' she said witheringly.

'My last nagging doubt is soothed.' He sighed with ostentatious relief.

She sucked in her breath with indignation; he was a smug rat. 'You're too insensitive ever to suffer a doubt,' she jeered. His confidence was as integral to him as the careless charm of his smile.

'I can't believe a sensual woman like you was willing to marry an unimaginative slob.'

'Alex isn't a slob; he's very particular about his clothes.'

Irritatingly so at times, she recalled. She tried to ignore the fact that Callum had called her sensual because it made her feel strangely vulnerable. 'Besides, I thought you didn't think love had anything to do with marriage,' she challenged.

'True, but to marry someone you don't find sexually attractive is just making life unnecessarily difficult. I notice you defended his sartorial elegance but didn't deny the lack of imagination. Any man who found you wanting in bed must be a complete clod! There's something about you that excites a man's fantasies, Georgina. A warmth and mystery…'

The flicker of his eyes as they moved over her tense face was hot and glittering. 'I didn't find the reality a disappointment,' he confided huskily. 'Or do you need anonymity before you can truly lose your inhibitions? Is that what turns you on?'

His crude speculation made her feel sick. She wasn't about to confess that he was the only man who had ever made her feel simultaneously abandoned and fulfilled. 'There's no fooling you, is there?' she taunted angrily. 'Who needs psychologists when we have Callum Stewart?'

'I might not be an expert, honey, but I can claim more insight than you appear to possess. You despise your mother… Why? For being a warm, generous woman, able to express her feelings? I don't think you're in any position to criticise.'

His contempt and disgust made her flinch. 'If being a warm, generous woman means crying yourself to sleep I'm quite content to skip that stage of development, thank you.' She could recall lying in her own bed, hearing her mother weeping long into the night, and it had always been a man that was to blame. She'd been stupid once, putting her trust in Alex, believing he was different. But Alex had proved he couldn't be trusted either and finding that out had hurt.

'I can see why you...or any man, for that matter...prefer warm, generous women,' she drawled caustically. 'Men are such dear, trustworthy little creatures—who can blame her or any other woman? I don't despise my mother—I pity her! I pity her for falling for men like you wheeling out tired old lines.'

'I don't recall ever skipping out on any female while she was asleep, Georgina.'

The glint of anger in his eyes made her lean back in her seat. 'What's wrong? Was I supposed to tell you how marvellous you were? Or did you just want to tell me what a fool I'd been?'

She'd never forgive him for making such a total idiot of her. He had manipulated her from the instant they'd met. God, she thought, looking around the restaurant with an incredulous frown, he's still doing it now. I should have just walked out and let him salvage Oliver's company. He's certainly devious enough to achieve anything, she thought as a rush of tears suddenly swam across her vision.

'I'm going home,' she announced, folding her napkin and placing it on the table. She rose hastily, sure of only one thing...she had to escape from his presence.

Callum followed her example and got to his feet. He silenced a concerned query from the waiter with a white-lipped glare. 'You're not going anywhere until I tell you,' he snapped.

Not up to his usual standard by any means... From anyone else such an ultimatum would have sounded foolish and absurd. It sounded neither on his lips, but he must have known that, short of forcing her, which was not really an option even in front of this politely incurious crowd, he couldn't stop her.

'I don't fancy your odds on that. For a hungry man, Callum, you don't each much. Why don't you sit down like a good boy and concentrate on your food? It might be easier to accept on a full stomach that I'm not about to become your sexual slave.'

He smiled suddenly and the flash of white teeth made alarm bells ring in her head. 'Sexual slave—mmm...' His voice had risen several decibels and she could almost see the ears around them pricking up to catch any more juicy slivers of conversation. 'I don't mind discussing our personal life in front of an audience,' he informed her, his temper becoming benign as her own began to sizzle.

'Shut up, Callum!' she whispered fiercely. 'I happen not to like being conspicuous.'

'A glowering goddess with hair like a burnished cloud is bound to get attention. I don't mind you glowering at me,' he confided in a husky tone. 'In fact,' he said with breathtaking frankness, 'I find it...stimulating.' He rolled the word thoughtfully over his tongue, caressing the syllables in a way that anchored her feet to the ground. 'Let's forget dinner and discuss our communication problem in less public surroundings.'

He walked around the table and placed the suggestion of a hand in between her shoulderblades. Even though several centimetres of air separated them she felt the touch like a red-hot brand. He must have noticed her involuntary shudder but he made no comment as together they left the room.

'I prefer to remain in public surroundings with you,' she managed huskily as she fought against the dragging sensation that stroked her senses into a state of quivering hunger. 'Why can't you just accept that what we had was a one-night stand and nothing else? I think we'd both be disappointed if we tried to resurrect what happened.'

Callum caught her arm and swung her around to face him. 'We have no trouble communicating when we don't talk. In fact, non-verbally, I think we've got the nearest thing to telepathy I've ever experienced.'

It didn't take three guesses to realise what particular form of non-verbal communication he was talking about. 'Sex is not the answer to everything.'

A glint of humour slid into his darkened blue eyes. 'It would make me feel one hell of a lot better at this particular moment,' he admitted candidly. 'You must know you're driving me crazy!' he added, rotating his neck slowly as if to relieve tension. It was true—wanting her was becoming an obsession. He told himself it was the chase that was bewitching him. Once he'd reached his goal he'd be able to work her out of his system.

'You did mention I'm a distraction.' The sort of relationship he had in mind had a built-in obsolescence for her. The hunt...the capture—that was all part of the game for him. Once the novelty wore off he'd move on. All they had in common was sexual attraction.

I want more...so much more. She acknowledged the fact with reluctance. The ache of steel-edged frustration inside made her wonder whether she had the strength not to accept what he was offering, and to hell with the consequences.

'So you are,' he agreed ruefully. He reached out and touched the fine mesh of her hair. The movement had all the hallmarks of compulsion about it. He watched the light dancing along the tawny fibres as they slipped through his fingers, almost as if he'd forgotten how they came to be there, and she saw the muscles in his throat work hard as he swallowed. 'I'm not into self-denial as wholeheartedly as you are. Do you like driving men a little crazy?'

Crazy? Me? She thought of her not quite pretty face and not quite slim enough figure and tried to see if he was mocking her. No, there was no sign of humour in his set features. 'Men?'

'Simon May, my uncle...'

'Simon hates me, I think, and your uncle was never...'

She coloured self-consciously and glared at him indignantly. 'He was always the perfect gentleman.'

'Probably what sent him to an early grave,' Callum mused callously.

'What a totally disgusting thing to say!'

Callum's lips twisted in an obdurate grimace. 'Foul and repellent,' he agreed. 'But accurate. For once in your life be honest and accept you want the same thing I do. Do you need to justify your urge to mate, Georgina?' he asked, his voice as insidiously caressing as a swirling current in dangerous waters. Did being in love mean you had to allow yourself to drown? The nature of her thoughts made her freeze. I don't love Callum Stewart! She screamed the words within the confines of her skull.

'Do you want me to talk of love and commitment?' And for one awful moment she thought the words had left her lips. 'Your faithful Alex did all those things. Don't put your faith in words; accept instinct. Every instinct is telling you to come with me, isn't it?'

She'd forgotten the casual passers-by in the foyer and the focal point that the tableau of their immobile figures made. His voice and the wild response it was evoking were all she was aware of. 'You're asking me to put my faith in you?' I must be mad to even consider this! she thought.

'Cal!' The cheery hail made Callum spin around, a dark scowl on his features. 'Thought we'd be too early.' A tall young man with collar-length blond hair and a square jaw identical to Callum's slapped him enthusiastically on the shoulder. 'Introduce us to the lovely lady,' he demanded in an attractive accent more pronounced than Callum's.

'Hello again.' As Georgina tried to regain her composure—the transition to reality was bewildering after the intense concentration of moments before—the dark girl of earlier that day moved into her line of vision. 'I did try to hold him back,' she said softly, her voice apologetic, 'but tact and discretion are not my husband's strongest points. Hi, Cal, darling… My, doesn't he look delighted to see us, Rick?'

She hugged Callum and with a rueful bark of laughter he responded, relaxing his broad shoulders as he hugged the girl, but his eyes when they met Georgina's were seething with frustration.

'Is this a bad time?' With a puzzled expression Rick looked from Georgina to his brother.

Tricia, once more replaced on her feet, let out a crow of laughter. 'When they handed out intuition he was at the end of the queue, poor lamb,' she observed drily. 'Do you want a drink, Cal, or shall I drag him off?'

Her forthright approach and the dawning curiosity in Rick's grey eyes were making Georgina acutely uncomfortable. 'Actually I should be going,' she murmured faintly.

The young couple's admonitions were sliced neatly by Callum's incisive 'No!'

Georgina felt her temper surge into life. Where did he get off with all that you'll-jump-when-I-speak rubbish? she thought, her eyes smouldering dangerously.

'Very masterful, Cal,' his brother observed in a voice that didn't hide his curiosity at this unusual behaviour.

'Rude and arrogant were my thoughts on the subject,' Georgina said, recovering her voice.

'Too true…but then he's always had leanings in that direction,' the young man explained, ignoring his brother's murderous glare. 'What's your name? You seem like a woman with sense and discrimination,' he continued, placing an inoffensive arm across her shoulders. 'What are you doing with my brother?'

The charm was of a totally different type from Callum's and, completely unintimidated, she found herself responding to the twinkling eyes and outrageous wink.

'I'm Georgina Campion.'

'Come on, Georgina Campion, and have a drink with my wife and me; we're celebrating.' He gave his elder brother a passing glance. 'You can come too,' he offered in a spirit of generosity.

Somehow Georgina found herself led to the lounge bar and seated in the middle of the Stewart clan. Rick was exuberant and his young wife drily humorous. The young couple appeared to have accepted her as though she and Callum were an item—a fact she found distinctly unsettling. It would be nice if the scenario were true, she thought wistfully, her eyes drawn to Callum's face as he laughed at some outrageous comment his brother had made.

'Are you here on holiday?' she asked, swallowing hard as Callum intercepted her look. The sardonic gleam in his eyes made her heart rate quicken alarmingly. At times it was difficult to believe that he couldn't read minds. She felt emotionally exposed with him in a way she'd never experienced before.

'Delayed honeymoon,' Tricia said, with a quick, intimate smile at her husband. 'The first moment we've been able to get away; Wollundra is this one's mistress,' she said with mock censure. Her confidence made it clear that that situation was anything but true.

'Have you been married long?' Georgina quashed a surge of jealousy at the obvious warmth in their relationship. It made her poignantly aware of what she was missing out on, and how much had been missing from her relationship with Alex.

'Three years…'

'Two months, five days and—' Rick glanced at his wristwatch '—five hours, twenty-seven minutes.' He reached out his hand and clasped his wife's, raising it to his lips.

'How is Susie?' Callum asked.

'Mum's the same as ever; she sends you her love and says when are you coming home, brother. I told her you were too busy playing a big tycoon. Have you got that situation under control, Callum?'

'I'm working on it,' Callum said, slanting Georgina a lazily speculative look.

'He was quite a character, Oliver,' Rick mused with a grin. 'You could tell he was Ruth's brother straight away. He turned up at Wollundra a few years back to give Callum the once-over,' he explained to Georgina. 'It was a regular royal visitation, just like her ladyship, but he brought his personal assistant instead of his hairdresser.' He laughed and slapped his thigh. 'If you'll pardon the expression, I've seen belts longer than the skirts she wore and—'

'I think I should point out before you get yourself in any deeper, brother, that until his death Georgina was Oliver's PA,' Callum put in blandly.

Rick's mouth opened and closed twice before he actually spoke. 'Anyone got a crowbar to get this foot out of my mouth?' he asked hopefully. 'No offence intended, Georgina.'

'Don't worry, Rick, I've weathered worse insults recently,' she said, giving Callum a very pointed glare.

'What was she called, Rick?' Callum enquired.

'Miss Jones,' Rick replied uncomfortably.

'That was it…' Callum agreed with a reminiscent grin. 'Oliver did have an eye for a good pair of…legs. Mind you, Georgina wears her skirts much longer—at least at work. In fact it's almost like a uniform with her hair scraped back, not to mention her glasses. Do you actually need them?' he asked her.

'I'm very short-sighted.'

'That explains why she's out with you, big brother,' Rick put in.

'This is business,' Georgina responded too quickly. The younger Stewart regarded her with amused scepticism and the older with a virtuous expression that made her grit her teeth.

'It must have been interesting working for Oliver.'

Georgina smiled gratefully at Tricia. 'It was,' she agreed. 'I miss him.' Let them make what they like of that, she thought, lifting her chin.

'Georgina held a very privileged position in the agency. It must be hard to take it when you see your influence eroded.'

'What I meant was I miss Oliver as a person,' she said, longing to wipe that supercilious sneer off his face.

'Have you got something in your eye, Georgina?' Callum asked, examining the sudden misty sheen in her eyes with cynical distaste.

'Only my contact lenses,' she responded grimly.

Rick, encouraged by his wife's grimaces and the kick on his shin, broke the awkward pause. 'Mum was over the moon when I gave her the good news. I've told her she'll have to mend her ways if she's going to be a grandmother.'

'Your smugness borders on the nauseous,' Callum observed, his lips twitching slightly as he shifted his attention from Georgina. 'You'd think no one ever produced a baby before.'

'Naturally not one as talented and exceptionally beautiful as ours will be,' his brother responded.

'You two are embarrassing Georgina,' Tricia remonstrated. 'Callum hadn't told you, Georgina?'

Just what sort of relationship did they think she had with Callum? she wondered, imagining how different their attitude would be if they knew how their paths had crossed. If they knew she had been a one-night stand!

'It came as a bit of a surprise to us too; I thought I'd developed air sickness,' Tricia recalled, her dark eyebrows shooting up towards her hairline. 'I've got so used to Rick announcing my condition to the whole world, I just took it for granted... Callum has more discretion.'

'Congratulations,' Georgina murmured warmly. That glow was easily explainable now. Would their child have the Stewarts' obstinate chin? she wondered, unaware of the wistful smile that tugged at her lips.

'Feeling broody, Georgina?' Rick joked. 'Have to watch out, brother.' He appeared oblivious to the sudden drop in temperature around the table.

'Georgina is a career woman, Rick. I don't think maternal feelings keep her awake nights.'

She could see by the tightening of the muscles along his jawline that Callum hadn't liked his brother's light-hearted remark. The assumption that she didn't want children...wasn't fit to have them was probably what he meant...made her stiffen. His acrid observation might not have been meant to wound but it had cut her deeply.

I'm overreacting here, she reasoned, lowering her eyes over the hurt and anger. But the pain still didn't retreat. 'Can't career women become mothers?' she enquired, lifting her head with a jerk. Her hair lashed across her face as she tossed back her head, and she brushed it impatiently out of her eyes.

'You make choices in life. A mother who bears a child just because she doesn't want to miss out on the experience is being selfish in the worst possible way. Something has to give, and for women like you it's not going to be the job, is it?'

The uncomfortable silence was broken by Tricia. 'It's only men who can't juggle, Callum. Women have been doing it for years,' she said lightly. 'Besides, I'm all for sharing. Rick is keen to experience the joys of nappies.'

'I am?'

'Women like me?' Georgina said in a dangerous voice, totally ignoring Tricia's pacific comment. Callum's arrogant presumption went beyond all bounds. 'Don't stop now; I'm agog to hear what sermon you're choking on. Tell me, do they engrave your observations on the meaning of life in stone?'

A suspicious sound escaped Rick's throat, but it was cut off when his wife sent him a warning glance.

'All through history there have been examples of women defending their offspring against tremendous odds. What is less well documented is the fact that others have no maternal instincts whatever and those women should not have children. I'm not saying it's a modern phenomenon.'

The cold silver light that filtered into his blue eyes made him appear more remote than a total stranger. He was too intelligent to believe all that sexist rubbish, surely? she thought incredulously. 'It was a sad day when we got the vote,' she said sympathetically, her eyes glowing with scorn.

'There's no need to take it personally.'

'Like hell there isn't!' she snarled back. She got to her feet with unconscious dignity. 'I'm not your mother, Callum Stewart, so don't work out your aggression on me. My maternal feelings, or lack of them, are none of your damned business. In fact,' she said flatly, 'nothing I do is.'

What an exit line, she thought. Swallowing a bubble of hysteria, she walked away. He didn't try to stop her but, having seen the violent surge of icy rage that contorted his features when she'd mentioned his mother, she hadn't expected him to.

Before she got into her cab Tricia came running up. The girl looked at her with deep concern in her dark eyes. 'Don't go, Georgina,' she begged.

'Did Callum ask you to say that? I thought not,' she said, when the other girl's expression spoke volumes.

'I know he was wildly out of order. He may not be a modern man exactly,' she conceded, 'but he likes women.' She looked genuinely confused. 'You touched a bit of a nerve about his mother.'

Georgina drew in a deep breath and looked the girl straight in the eye. 'He doesn't *like* me, Tricia. He wants to sleep with me…against his better judgement.'

'Do you like him?'

Georgina swallowed the solid lump of emotion that rose in her throat. She shook her head helplessly. 'No, but I do…' She went deathly pale as she realised what she'd been about to admit. Not him, not Callum—fate couldn't be that cruel! She gave the driver her instructions and slid inside. The realisation made her feel sick. How could she have let it happen? Why me? she wondered with the age-old cry of bewilderment.

She didn't need to say it out loud to Tricia; she could see sympathy on the other woman's face. She must be painfully transparent. She felt reasonably confident that Tricia wouldn't betray the confidence; they'd established an unusual rapport, considering the short length of their acquaintance. She hunched her shoulders as silent tears slid down her cheeks. What could she do when circumstances were so totally out of control?

CHAPTER EIGHT

GEORGINA STARTED as her mother returned to the small sitting room carrying a tray. Turning her back on the idyllic rural scene through the window, she took a seat. Best china. Mother always did have a sense of occasion. Her daughter's presence, Georgina thought guiltily, had become rare enough for her to realise that there was nothing casual about this visit.

Georgina didn't protest as sugar was liberally spooned into her cup, despite the fact that she'd stopped taking any in her teens. Once the action would have irritated her intensely but now, with more important things on her mind, she let it pass.

'You've left your job. Was that wise?'

Peter Llewellyn had asked her to stay on once she'd worked her six weeks' notice. She'd been touched and pleased by his enthusiasm to keep her on. 'It was necessary,' Georgina returned, balancing a biscuit on her saucer. 'I've got good references.' Glowing would be more accurate. When she was in a position to look for a job once more she was going to be grateful for that. 'I've signed on with a temp agency at the moment.'

'But you are looking for something permanent?'

Georgina took a deep breath. 'In theory pregnancy shouldn't make a difference to a prospective employer. In reality it can prove an obstacle,' she said drily. 'It's never the reason they give, but…'

A slight flinch and a widening of the expertly made-up

eyes were the only outward signs that her mother had registered her news. Georgina, who had been expecting, with resignation, a general beating of breasts and tearing out of hair, relaxed fractionally. Perhaps this wasn't going to be as bad as she had expected.

'Are you keeping it?'

'Yes!' The vehemence made the older woman blink.

'So, I'm to be a grandmother. More tea?'

An incredulous smile tilted the corners of Georgina's generous lips. 'You never fail to amaze me,' she observed.

'On this occasion the amazement is all mine. I take it you'll clam up if I mention the father? I thought so,' Lydia said as a faint spasm of pain contorted her daughter's features. 'In that case, I won't ask,' she said briskly. 'I'll stick to practicalities. Are you planning to move back here?'

Georgina thought she detected relief when she shook her head. Who could blame her mother? The small cottage had two bedrooms and one of them barely fitted her single bed. Support had been the last thing she had expected but she was getting it—quiet, non-judgemental support. The sense of relief not to be completely alone was intense.

The last six weeks had been one of the most confusing periods of her life as she'd suspected and then known for sure that she was carrying Callum's child. Above and beyond the fear and confusion she had discovered a strong, unexpected core of happiness. She hadn't realised how strong it was until her GP had bluntly asked her the same question her mother had. Then she had known how deeply she did want this child. She'd gone from feeling weighed down with the burden of her new responsibilities to experiencing the most incredibly protective urges of a prospective mother.

'I'll keep my flat.'

'How will you manage...financially?' A crease of worry pleated her mother's still smooth brow.

'You did.'

'Is the father going to contribute?' Lydia said, relief in her voice. 'Your father never shirked his duty, Georgina; my job in the florist's wouldn't have kept us.'

Georgina's gaze shifted uncomfortably. She couldn't tell her mother how impossible it was for her to let Callum know about the baby. How could she expect commitment when all that had been between them had been physical? She had no right to compel him to accept an unwanted child, and under the circumstances she felt she owed him anonymity. The fact that she'd fallen in love didn't alter the superficial nature of their brief relationship.

'Actually, Oliver left me a legacy,' she admitted eventually. She knew she couldn't afford to prove her moral superiority and not touch the windfall now. Besides, such a gesture would be lost on Callum; he probably hadn't given her a thought. This one time he'd been to London she'd only known because Peter had mentioned it in passing. It put things painfully in perspective, with the emphasis on pain!

Her mother went white. 'Are you trying to tell me that Oliver...?' She clutched her throat as if she was having trouble breathing. 'He wouldn't!' she said in a strangled voice.

'Mother!' Georgina cried, outraged. 'Not you too!' Her annoyance turned to concern as a faint blue discoloration etched Lydia's lips. 'Can I get you something...a brandy?'

'No, no, I'm fine.'

'You don't look it,' Georgina said frankly. This was more the reaction she'd expected earlier in the conversation. 'Oliver left me a stack of shares, and, before you ask me why, don't. I've no more idea than you.' The brown manila envelope had contained nothing more than the share certificates—no note, nothing. This bizarre generosity was still a mystery to her.

'You're wrong, my dear; I do have an idea—a very good idea.'

'You do...?' Perplexed by this statement, Georgina stared at her grim-faced parent.

'Before I met your father I knew Oliver Mallory. I knew him very well.' She eyed her daughter almost apprehensively.

Georgina sat in stunned silence. 'Why didn't you say when I went to work for him?'

'Because I asked Oliver to give you the clerical job.'

'You mean I became his personal assistant because you once slept with him?' Georgina choked.

'No...no, I didn't interfere after that. He wouldn't have given you the first chance if you hadn't been up to it,' she said urgently, kneading her elegant hands in anguish. 'Oliver never was one to tolerate incompetence.' She gave a small, brittle laugh. 'It's just that I wanted to give you a head start; you seemed to want it so badly. There were so many who were just as qualified as you were... I just wanted to help.'

Georgina raised her fingers to her temples and shook her head, still trying to assimilate these revelations. 'He remembered you after all those years?'

'We didn't have a casual affair, Georgie; I almost married him.'

'You and Oliver...' she mumbled in disbelief. 'He wasn't my...?' She swallowed, not quite able to say the word.

'Father?' Lydia gave a bitter laugh. 'No, he wasn't. But he might well have been if things had worked out differently. Oliver was a very ambitious man,' she recalled. 'He felt a wife and children at that stage in his career would slow him down. I gave him an ultimatum; in my youthful arrogance I thought he'd choose me.' Her voice cracked with emotion. 'Oliver was always in a hurry,' she reflected, with a small, bitter smile that spoke volumes.

Georgina felt a surge of compassion, feeling closer to her mother than she ever had before.

'I married your father, had you, and then Oliver came back. We resumed where we'd left off.'

Georgina felt a lot less shocked than she would have a few weeks before. 'Did Father know?'

'Oliver made sure he did. He could be quite ruthless and he wanted me to leave your father and…you. I couldn't.' She blinked back tears and, reaching for her handkerchief, sniffed delicately into it. 'I never saw him again after the final row and we tried, your father and I, to patch things up, but he never really forgave me and he left. So, you see, in his own way—the only way he knew how—Oliver was trying to make up for what he did to us.'

'I thought Dad left because of me,' Georgina said, her voice almost suspended by tears.

'I know it was selfish of me to let you think that but I knew how badly you'd think of me if you knew the truth. It wasn't as if Paul didn't want to keep in touch. He was working abroad and when he came back he had his new family to consider.'

'I was surplus to requirements.'

'No, darling, it wasn't that; it's just he felt a stranger after all those years. He always remembered his financial commitment to us.'

Knowing this might have helped all those years ago when she'd felt abandoned and obscurely responsible. But it was too late to speculate now and too late to know her father, she thought sadly; he had died three years before.

'I never contacted Oliver all those years, or asked him for anything until you were looking for a job…I swear!'

Georgina had fallen to her knees on the hearth rug to catch the soft words. She reached out, and her mother, after

a moment's hesitation, caught her hands. Georgina found
it was she offering the comfort as they hugged.

These revelations made her see the past in quite a different light. She was learning that things were never as
black and white as they appeared. Her father hadn't just
upped and left without an explanation, and her mother,
whom she'd always imagined to be the most superficial
person she knew, had spent years trying to forget a tragic
love affair in the arms of other men.

They talked more than they ever had done before that
afternoon, but by an unspoken agreement neither mentioned the men in their lives.

The only person at Mallory's who knew about the baby
was Mary. Dear, discreet and supportive Mary, Georgina
thought affectionately. These days her social contacts were
slender; the temp work had dried up now that her pregnancy was well advanced and she missed the stimulation
of work. She looked forward to the evenings she spent with
the older woman and her husband. Their teenage children
periodically appeared between their own hectic social ar-
rangements and she watched with a mixture of envy and
bewilderment the dynamics of a large family. Her own
childhood seemed stark in contrast to the loud altercations
and noisy jokes.

Georgina glanced at her watch. Mary must be working
late. She was waiting as arranged in the underground car
park at Mallory's. She could imagine the comments her
presence would provoke if she chose to walk through the
building right now. Her hand went to the expanding mound
of her belly, no longer disguised by the oversized shirt and
cardigan she wore.

If news of her condition should reach the wrong ears…
An expression of cold determination hardened her features.
Would Callum even acknowledge his relationship to the

unborn child? She didn't want to know, she thought grimly. This was her baby! He'd already implied she was basically unfit to be a mother; she wasn't letting him have any say in the matter.

'Well, well, well!'

She jumped as if stung. 'Simon!' Her heart dropped as she looked around the empty basement, hoping to see Mary.

'Come back to grovel for your old job?'

Even before he got nearer Georgina could see that he was drunk. 'I'm waiting for someone,' she said shortly.

'Mr Great-and-bloody-perfect Stewart, I s'pose...' he slurred.

The knowledge that Callum was in the building filled Georgina with a panic that made her blind to the insulting way the man's eyes were running over her body. Simon dropped his car keys on the floor as he lurched closer and the noise drew Georgina's attention back to her immediate predicament.

'I hope you're not going to drive in that condition,' she said, her nostrils flaring in distaste as the raw smell of alcohol wafted towards her when he straightened up.

'Hope you're not going to drive like that,' he mimicked. 'I'll do what I bloody well like. Do you hear me? You stuck-up little...!'

Georgina let out a startled shriek as he lunged forward and caught her by the hair. His velocity sent her hard against Mary's car. The contact of his heavy body made her feel like retching.

'Let go of me!' she yelled, turning her head to one side to avoid the malicious glitter of his eyes. But she knew it would be fatal to show any fear; a man like this would feed on it. He was leaning heavily against her, against her baby. She wanted to scream but there was no one to hear her. She had to protect the baby!

'Too good for me, weren't you? Well, I'm calling the shots now.'

He twisted his fingers in her hair, and his mouth, wet and hot, covered hers. Her body was rigid with rejection and shock. Instinctively she bit down hard on his lip, revolted and terrified by the assault. Simon lifted his head, cursing as he touched the blood dripping from his mouth. Raising his arm, he struck her, backhanded, across the cheek, sending her head sideways. He would have done it again to stop her screams if he hadn't been lifted bodily off her.

Georgina slid to the floor as her legs collapsed beneath her, numb and shaking. Mary was there beside her before the noises of the brief scuffle stopped.

'Something's wrong,' she said. Her eyes were darkly tragic as she lifted her head off the other woman's shoulder. 'The baby...' she said, her voice shaking with fear.

'Is she all right?' Callum materialised at their side. He was rubbing the grazed knuckles of his right hand and his face looked like thunder.

'We need an ambulance,' Mary replied urgently.

'What did the bastard do?'

'No, it's the baby,' Mary said, running a soothing hand over Georgina's clammy forehead.

Callum froze, and went an unhealthy grey beneath his dark tan. His eyes moved over the still form of the girl slumped on the floor until they reached the definite expansion around her middle.

'No time; we'll use my car,' he said, life suddenly returning to his limbs. He bent down and scooped Georgina up. She felt as limp as a rag doll in his arms. Her waxen eyelids flickered open and for a moment their eyes met; she looked at him blankly as if she didn't recognise him.

The journey to the hospital was a blur. She knew Mary was beside her and that she kept saying comforting things, but Georgina was convinced that something too terrible for words to make better was happening. Mary gasped occasionally as the car made some unorthodox manoeuvre through the heavy traffic but Georgina was oblivious to all external matters.

Callum carried her into the casualty department, undeterred by official attempts to halt his progress. She didn't know what he said or did, but very soon she was in a cubicle, being seen by a distinguished-looking man with a carnation in his lapel.

His hands moved clinically over her body and his smile was professionally noncommittal. 'Pain?'

'Not now,' she said flatly. 'My baby's dead, isn't it?' she said hoarsely.

'Did your companion do that?' he asked sternly, touching the bruised side of her face.

Georgina looked at him with frustration; she wasn't concerned about her face. 'Callum?' she asked with amazement. 'Of course not!' she said indignantly, colouring as she realised the direction her thoughts were going. 'There was a drunk in the car park.'

'In that case I'll let him in whilst we listen for the heartbeat,' he said, his manner visibly relaxing. 'Security will be relieved,' he observed wryly, half to himself.

'The baby's alive...?' she said incredulously. She was too relieved to tell him that Callum didn't belong here at all. When the electronic monitor picked up the swift sounds of the baby's heartbeat it was the sweetest music she'd ever heard. She closed her eyes and large, silent tears ran down her face. She didn't look at Callum quietly standing in the corner of the tiny room.

'But I was bleeding,' she said as her anxiety returned.

'A very slight loss; no need to panic. We'll send you for a scan immediately. Then I'll see you on the ward a little later.'

She gave a quivering sigh and smiled faintly. 'Thank you.'

The doctor disappeared behind the curtain and they were alone. Just the two of us—no, three, she thought, her hand going to her stomach in a protective gesture. She turned her head slowly to look at him, defiance and caution in her eyes.

He looked so bleak, so incredibly grim that she shuddered apprehensively. It was impossible to tell what he was thinking. 'I... Thank you for getting rid of Simon; you can go now. Tell Mary I'm all right, will you?'

'Thank you for giving me permission,' he drawled with savage sarcasm, 'but I'll go when I damned well want to and not before. You know they thought I'd attacked you?' he said, disgust curling his upper lip. 'What in God's name possessed you to start seeing May? I wouldn't have thought you'd believe in rekindling old flames.'

She blinked, startled by the explosive question. 'I wasn't—'

'You were waiting for him in the bloody car park. Pregnant. How stupid and thoughtless can you get? A man who beats you and you get pregnant. If you want to put yourself in that position, fine! But exposing a child to that sort of abuse is criminally irresponsible!'

It was ironic when she considered how terrified she'd been of him finding out about the baby. He actually thought she and Simon... She ought to feel relief but she felt a lick of pure rage. How dared he think she...? She had quite absurdly expected him to know instinctively that the child was his and perversely she felt furious with him for not realising it.

'I'll naturally cherish your opinion,' she drawled, shaking with reaction. She'd forgotten how intensely blue his eyes were; they were cold and furious but still capable of making her stomach tighten.

She despised her weakness, aware of the danger it represented. Even now she was conscious of every minute detail of his appearance—the way his hair curled against his collar, the shadow his eyelashes cast along the slant of his cheekbones. Concentrate, Georgie, she told herself, lowering her gaze with an enormous effort. 'Go and tell Mary; she'll be worried.' And she gave a sigh of relief when, amazingly, he did as she requested.

Callum calmly walked into the room just as the technician was beginning the scan. 'Sorry I'm late; I was getting Mary a taxi. I told her I'd keep her up to date with any news.'

The technician smiled, accepting his right to be there. Georgina could have wept with frustration; she ought to have known he'd been too uncharacteristically docile in disappearing. She could have made a fuss and had him expelled but she couldn't take her eyes off the screen. She had to know if everything was all right!

'Sit here; you'll be able to see better,' the young woman said helpfully.

This was too much! Georgina had just turned her head to glare at him when the girl's next words glued her eyes to the screen.

'There's the heart beating…just there.'

Georgina was hooked as the commentary continued, fascinated by the grainy images on the screen. Words like bonding took on a new meaning as the emotions rose within her and tears welled in her eyes. 'Is everything all right?'

She relaxed at the cheerful reply, her tears obscuring her vision. She turned her head and discovered Callum's chest. It seemed the most natural thing in the world to seek comfort in hard solidity. For a few moments she burrowed, clutching at handfuls of his shirt with trembling fingers.

His fingers were in her hair, kneading the strained muscles of her neck.

'Let me see, you must be twenty-nine weeks by now,' the girl observed, oblivious to the sudden tension in the room. Georgina straightened up, not daring to look at Callum. A frisson of pure dread lanced through her.

'No, I...I don't think so,' Georgina stammered, trying desperately to retrieve the situation. She couldn't hope that Callum hadn't picked up on that; he was far too astute not to draw the obvious conclusions from this fact.

'You'd be amazed how many people don't have their dates right,' the girl said with a laugh, wiping the gel off Georgina's stomach and readjusting the white hospital gown. 'But the measurements give a very accurate estimate.'

He didn't say a word—just gave one fierce, accusatory glare. Anticipation of what he would say was almost worse than the actual event; she could read menace in every line of his body. The baby is alive—that's all that matters, she kept telling herself.

She was tucked up in bed by the time the doctor reappeared. 'Let's have Dad in on this, shall we?' he said cheerfully, and Georgina almost groaned out loud as Callum appeared on cue.

The technical details were vaguely confusing but Georgina hung onto the words 'no reason why you shouldn't have a perfectly healthy baby'. The mention of total bed rest for two weeks and careful monitoring made her thoughts become frantic as she pondered with dismay the practical implications of this news.

The obvious solution was to go home, but her mother had never really been good at the nursemaid side of maternal responsibility. She had been a firm believer in illness being very much a question of mind over matter. As far

as Georgina could recall, a brisk walk had been her answer
to most of the childish ailments she had suffered.

'I'll see she looks after herself and the baby.'

Georgina shot Callum a startled look. Circumstances
and the fact that she'd been too gutless and embarrassed
to tell the doctor she didn't want him here might have
meant that Callum had been privy to this consolation but
she'd have to make it plain to him that his involvement
ended here.

'I'll see you both in the morning,' the doctor said, leaving them.

'I didn't know consultants were so accessible,' she observed with a frown as he closed the door. She looked
around the room with sudden suspicion. 'Why aren't I in
the main ward?'

'I thought you'd prefer some privacy.'

'I can't afford to pay for privacy.' Her voice felt thick
where her mouth was beginning to swell. I must look quite
awful, she thought, touching the bruised skin experimentally and wincing.

'I can,' he said, his expression tightening as he watched
her grimace of pain. 'And as it's my child we're talking
about it's my right. You have a peculiar view about my
rights, don't you, Georgina?' he accused her grimly. 'Did
you ever intend telling me?'

His softly furious question stilled her instinctive protest
at being in any way in his debt. 'It's none of your business,' she said stubbornly, covertly studying his face to
judge the degree of anger in his reaction to learning he
was to be a father. What she saw didn't make her feel any
more comfortable.

'My child is none of my business?' The fact that he
didn't raise his voice only served to emphasise his anger.
His blue eyes glittered ferociously.

'Biologically you're the father,' she admitted hoarsely.

'But your part was over with a long time ago. What we had was casual, a brief moment of madness.' Despite the sensation of dread that crawled in the pit of her stomach she tried to sound as impersonal and sensible as possible. I can't be seen to waver, she told herself firmly.

Callum's head jerked as though she'd struck him but his face was as hard as rock. 'The baby changes things.'

'Not for you.'

'You can't really think I'm willing to let you deny me contact with my child?'

'I find your possessive attitude a little difficult to take,' she snapped, feeling close to exhaustion by this point. 'Until a few minutes ago you didn't know the child existed and you cared less.'

'And whose fault is that?'

'I want this child and you're not going to take him from me!' Knuckles clenched bone-white on the counterpane, she glared at him defiantly.

'What the hell are you talking about?' he grated, looking only marginally more in control than she did.

'I'm not fit to be a mother. I haven't forgotten what you said. Well, if you think I'm going to let you take this child away from me, you're wrong! Just because you have money it doesn't mean you can buy everything.' Furiously she wiped the tears from her cheeks with the back of her hand. 'Oh, pass me a tissue, will you?'

Callum produced a handkerchief from his pocket and sat down on the edge of the bed. 'Calm down,' he said gently. 'I don't think it can be good for you to get so upset.'

'You're the one trying to steal my baby.'

He blotted the dampness from her cheeks and looked at her with a curious expression she didn't understand. 'You really do want this baby, don't you? I accept that. I don't know where you've got these ludicrous notions about me separating you. But it's my child too and you can't cut me off. It's in both our interests to behave in a civilised fashion so don't force me to play rough, Georgina.'

'Is that a threat?' she asked hoarsely.

Callum made an impatient gesture. 'Nothing so dramatic. I'm not Simon May,' he said caustically. 'You've no right to attempt to keep me from my child. As things stand, you'll need help.

'Just shut up and listen,' he continued sternly, cutting off her protests. 'Who else is there? Simon May?' His expression hardened. 'You've got to agree not to see him again. A man who hits a woman never changes,' he observed with biting scorn. 'Did he think the child was his?' he asked thickly.

'I don't care what he thinks, or what you think!' she yelled back.

'Did you know he's been selling information to our main rival?'

Georgina just looked at him blankly. She couldn't believe he could actually think she was interested in the man. 'Has he?' she said flatly. Simon May was low on her agenda of interesting subjects.

'He got the push today, and he probably found out that our rivals are less keen on employing someone who's already sold out one employer than he imagined. I expect you took the full force of his frustration. Keep away from him!' he warned grimly. His gaze rested on the swollen, discoloured area across her jaw and he grimaced. 'Even if you don't have enough self-respect to know he's bad news, you've got to think about the baby. I'll have no compunction about making sure you don't keep it if you put its life in danger.'

'How dare you lecture me on responsibility?' she breathed wrathfully. His contemptuous assumption made her blood boil. He seemed to think she was in the middle of some torrid affair. If it hadn't been so offensive it would have been funny! 'You weren't very responsible when we conceived this child. Besides, I'm seven months pregnant. I hardly think my love life is something that need concern you.'

'You're a very sensual woman and being pregnant hasn't altered that,' he said in a clipped tone. 'I believe some women even find their appetites increase at these times.' The light in his blue eyes as they ran almost compulsively over her made her heart thud. 'I think you look beautiful and desirable.'

He raised his hand to his forehead and closed his eyes. She saw the muscles in his throat work as he swallowed. 'You'd better sleep, Georgina,' he said heavily, getting up. He scribbled down a number on a pad and ripped off the paper. 'If you need anything ring me. I'll contact your mother and let her know what's going on.'

Callum took charge and Georgina was in no position to argue. The room was filled with fresh flowers every day, a gesture which might have meant something if she hadn't been convinced that Mary did this on his behalf.

He'd gained an ally in her mother, whom he'd housed in a luxurious hotel for the duration of her daughter's stay in hospital. Lydia visited her every day and was full of praise for him. She couldn't understand her daughter's stubborn rejection of the father of her child. In her opinion Callum was everything any woman could wish for and the way she dropped heavy hints concerning weddings when he was present made Georgina want to curl up and die from pure embarrassment.

What could she say? That he'd tricked her and she'd thought he was an escort hired by the hour? She couldn't defend her behaviour to anyone else when she still found it inexplicable. She still had some pride left! Despite Callum's reassurances she felt uneasy, convinced he wanted this child minus its mother.

Callum came every day, the perfect, attentive father, and only Georgina knew how deceptive appearances were. The last evening of her stay they sat in uncomfortable silence for half an hour. She gazed blankly at the pages of a glossy magazine, giving monosyllabic replies to all of his attempts to start a conversation.

'Cut it out, Georgina,' he said suddenly, removing the magazine from her fingers. 'You've proved your point—you don't like me,' he said heavily. He sat on the edge of the bed, his expression grave. 'I think it's time you started acting like a grown-up and thought about the future. We've got to put aside personal feeling and animosity and consider the child. He or she has to be the first consideration.'

Georgina's belligerent expression faded. The future was still something that frightened her. She hadn't wanted to think beyond the safety of the hospital bed.

'My childhood was disrupted by the wranglings of my parents. My mother never once stopped to think what effect her behaviour had on me. Even if Dad had taken the matter as far as court, in those days it was inevitable that the mother was given custody, unless the circumstances were extraordinary. Things are different now.'

'What are you trying to say?' she asked, going deathly pale. I should have known, she thought, swinging her legs over the side of the bed; he wants the baby without me...the unfit mother.

'What the hell are you doing?' he said, his fingers closing around her ankles. He lifted her legs back onto the bed and regarded her as if she'd taken leave of her senses.

'I won't let you take this baby away from me,' she said huskily, drawing her ankles up, away from the contact with his fingers.

Callum's mouth tightened as he surveyed her pale, tense

features. 'I wasn't talking about taking the child away, Georgina.'

She eyed him with distrust. 'You were quite voluble about my unfitness to be a mother.'

'One look at your face when you thought you were losing the baby was enough to make me realise I was wrong,' he said roughly.

Georgina stared at him in amazement. She could see he resented the admission, but at least he'd made it. Still, she wouldn't lower her defences.

'I was trying to say that a child needs a secure environment,' he continued. 'The last thing I'd subject any child of mine to would be being a pawn in a parental power game. A child needs both parents.'

Georgina trembled. What was he suggesting? 'A child wouldn't feel very secure with parents who actively disliked one another. You're not suggesting we stay together for the sake of the baby?' Her voice rose in shrill incredulity. 'My parents tried that for me, with painful consequences.'

'We're talking about us, not your parents. It seems the logical solution.'

'Who is refusing to learn from history now?' she accused him. It hurt that he could sound so pragmatic. Constantly required to live a lie...no, she couldn't bear it! 'It's an insane idea.'

'I'm not suggesting marriage,' he said, visibly impatient at her uncooperative attitude.

'Should I be grateful for small mercies?' she asked hoarsely.

'Save the sarcasm, Georgina,' he said, his face tight with anger. 'We've made a life between us and we have to adjust our own accordingly.'

Even if it didn't suit him, she added silently. He wanted

this child and she went with it. Feeling as she did, she couldn't risk constant exposure to him.

'You might find it's not so bad as you think,' he observed drily as he stared at her pale, drawn face. 'It would be hard for you as a single parent.'

'I've sold the shares Oliver left me,' she said, fighting against the moral blackmail he was so subtly applying. If she disagreed with him, she didn't have the baby's best interests at heart. If she did agree...wasn't there the possibility she wanted to agree just to stay close to him? 'I'll have more than a lot of single parents.'

'You should have waited a couple of months,' he said, his expression showing distaste at the mention of her inheritance. 'You'd have made more profit.'

Not as bad as she thought? It could only be worse! she thought wildly, not really hearing what he was saying. Not least because, to some self-destructive corner of her mind, the prospect of seeing him frequently was incredibly attractive. I'm pathetic, she thought, sick with self-disgust.

'I'll be back at work soon.' The logistics of that prospect were so mind-bogglingly difficult that she didn't feel any of the certainty expressed in her voice.

'If you're so anxious to continue your career, all the more reason to involve me. I can make it a lot easier for you to carry on up the slippery pole.'

'I can get where I want to be on my own merit.'

'An attitude which does you credit,' he said, his lip curling with contemptuous disbelief. She flushed at the implied insult. 'One way or another, Georgina, I *will* be part of this child's life. I make a bad enemy.' Smooth as a knifethrust, his words slid home.

She shivered; when he spoke like that it was hard to believe that everything he said wouldn't come to pass simply through the indomitable force of his will.

'You can't *want* to play happy families, Callum.'

'I want to do whatever I have to to give this child a stable environment,' he said heavily.

She stiffened as his hand reached out to cover her abdomen in a powerfully possessive gesture. The strange sensation that hit her made her feel light-headed. She had felt isolated lately by the things that were taking place in her own body. His touch made it feel as if she was sharing them for the first time. It wasn't entirely unpleasant, she realised as she lifted her dazed eyes to his face.

'You need me, Georgina; why is it so hard to admit it?' His blue eyes blazed with an intense emotion that she couldn't quite decipher. 'She moved.' His hands suddenly jerked clear.

'It's all right,' she said, catching his hand and guiding it back to her belly. 'You seem sure it's a girl.'

Callum's eyes gleamed with satisfaction at her instinctive gesture. 'I think she is,' he agreed softly. 'Let me look after you now?'

A frown between her brows, she lifted her troubled eyes to his. 'And later?'

'We'll work something out,' he promised. 'Take things one step at a time. Surely two intelligent people can come to a compromise?'

The trouble was, she reflected, that one of those intelligent people was in love, and being in love seemed to cancel out any claim to intellect that she'd ever possessed.

Despite her severe misgiving she found herself nodding. What alternative was there? She did have the baby to consider—about that much at least Callum was right. How long would it be before Callum discovered how she really felt about him? She shuddered to think how vulnerable that would make her. Well, I'll just have to make very sure he never finds out, she decided.

CHAPTER NINE

GEORGINA ARGUED but Callum appeared to have thought of every conceivable objection she might make to going with him to France. He managed to make every protest she made sound unreasonable and churlish. The trouble was that, practically speaking, he was right—she did need looking after. Her obstetrician had personally recommended a doctor in Montpellier, thus ruining her last remaining objection. She was passed fit to make the short journey and the wheels were set in motion.

'I seem to be the one making all the concessions here,' Georgina observed rattily as she perused the menu in the small café Callum had insisted they stop at on the journey from the airport. 'I can't even speak French.'

'You sound so *British* sometimes,' Callum observed with a faint smile.

'I should...I am—insular and uncompromising, that's me,' she replied, cheerfully selecting her meal and ordering in faltering French.

'Who am I to argue? Still, you managed that adequately so at least you won't starve,' he said drily, having ordered his own food in a much more fluent fashion.

'Ordering food is one thing, having a baby when no one understands what I'm saying is another.'

'A large proportion of the staff at the clinic speak English. We've been through all this, Georgina. I've arranged for a midwife to move in with us for the last two weeks.'

She made a disgruntled sound in her throat. Yes, he'd

been pretty comprehensive in his assumption that she was not capable of taking care of herself. 'I won't have anyone I *know*,' she complained, giving full range to the surge of self-pity.

'Your mother can stay; I've told you that. Besides, you'll know me.'

'Pardon me for not feeling comforted,' she snapped, her attention straying to a French family at a neighbouring table. Four generations, ranging from a septuagenarian to a toddler, settled down to eat together. She doubted whether children would have been welcomed quite so automatically in the British equivalent of this establishment.

'My mother is the last person I'd want at the birth,' she observed wistfully. Lydia had already advised Georgina to opt for the highest-tech birth available and her tales of her own horrifying experience were hardly designed to soothe her daughter's worries.

'Then, as I said, you'll have to do with me.'

She gave him a startled look. 'You want to be in at the birth?' She hadn't expected that and wasn't exactly sure how she felt about it. Callum was so possessive about the growing life within her that she almost felt jealous sometimes.

Longingly she wondered what it would be like to come under the cloak of his love. He was protective—extremely protective—but she knew this was only because she was carrying the child…his child. She didn't want to acknowledge the wave of emotion that washed over her. She'd be living in a fool's paradise if she read what she wanted to into his decision.

He raised his dark brows and shrugged. 'Of course I do.'

'But it's…intimate,' she said, struggling to express her doubts, suddenly fiercely embarrassed.

'So was the conception, as I recall,' he returned drily.

'Or does your memory need refreshing? I'm not playing at being a father, Georgina—I'm committed to the prospect.'

But not to me. She confronted the hurtful thought; sometimes it was only by remembering this painful truth that she could acknowledge the real situation between them. The knowledge that there was little about that night she'd ever forget made her colour and shift in her seat. 'I hardly think you'd enjoy that in my present condition,' she snapped, her jaw clenched.

'On the contrary, I'd enjoy it very much, but the doctor tells me that's a no-go area for the duration.'

'Why did he tell *you* that?' she asked in a scandalised voice. She knew, but he had no right telling Callum, she concluded with shaky logic.

'Because I asked.'

'You ask…!' Georgina choked. She was very grateful for the arrival of their food.

'Try this; it's a sort of chestnut casserole, a local speciality,' he explained, holding out his fork for her to sample the dish. 'Like it?' he enquired as she obligingly opened her mouth.

'Very nice,' she said primly, applying herself to her chicken dish. She realised that the casual gesture would have appeared intimate to anyone watching them. The problem was that it *was* intimate, just the two of them. She had no illusions he must resent her intrusion into his life; he was making the best of an impossible situation. 'I still don't see why I couldn't have stayed in England; you could have visited me there.'

Everything had happened so fast. If only she had been able to convince him she didn't need him, but the unpalatable fact was that she did. The doctor's tone had been alarming but the restrictions he had listed had been daunting.

'You're really tetchy,' Callum observed drily. 'Was the journey too much?' A crease of anxiety indented his forehead and his eyes searched her face intently. 'It's only an hour's drive to Ca'n D'alt, but we could stop here overnight if you prefer.'

'I'm fine,' she assured him. The flight to Toulouse had been smooth and the drive out of the city hadn't been taxing. Callum had made frequent stops for her to stretch her legs.

'I want to be involved with this child from the outset,' he said quietly. 'I don't want to be a weekend parent.'

'What about me—doesn't it matter what I want?' she asked in frustration.

'You need someone to make sure you slow down—'

'Nag me,' she interrupted mutinously. She had no intention of letting anything put her child at risk, no matter what he thought.

'For all I know you might have run back to May once the bruises had faded.'

Her lips remained firmly pressed together but her eyes flared with anger. 'That's my business,' she said coldly.

'Tell me about him.'

The perplexing order made her stare at him in confusion. 'I don't know what you mean.'

'I mean does he have a whole host of charming characteristics which are only apparent on closer acquaintance? You'd know all about them, wouldn't you, having such a *close* relationship? Or do you simply have a deeply masochistic streak? Are you attracted to brutes?' His voice was icy with derision.

'I never said I was having an affair with Simon—you did,' she reminded him.

'And are you telling me you weren't? Why else would you have been meeting him in the car park? That was hardly a chance encounter.'

'What's wrong—was your ego bruised at the idea of me hopping from your bed into someone else's?' she asked harshly. She had no intention of justifying herself to him when all he did was insult her. 'I thought you'd already decided I'd slept my way through the entire male staff at Mallory's,' she said bitterly.

She didn't want him to pursue this topic. If he realised how false his assumption about Simon was, it was conceivable he might guess how desperate she was to conceal the strength of her true feelings. So far she'd thankfully hidden her insecurity and ambiguous feelings behind his stupid misconception.

'In this condition that's one thing you won't have to worry about.' Her hand went to the firm mound of her belly. 'I'm as attractive as a stranded whale right now.'

The gesture drew his quickening gaze to her body. 'Were you angry with me when you found out?'

'Angry?' She looked at him blankly.

'You had your future so neatly planned; a child hardly fits in. It would only be natural for you to blame me.'

'Are you trying to get me to say I don't want this child so that you can take over?' she asked angrily.

He made an impatient noise in his throat. 'I know you want the child!' he said. 'I'm well aware that it's *me* you don't want, but that subject is not open to debate. In ideal circumstances a child should not be the result of a careless moment, but we're not living in an ideal world.'

'How profound,' she snapped. 'Does it say anything in your book of sage observations about what to do when the father of your child doesn't even exist? Callum Smith never did. I spent the night in question with him. The way I see it my baby doesn't have a father.'

'Immaculate conception it was not,' he retorted with a feral grin and a glint of hard anger in his eyes. 'I should have told you who I was; we should have used precautions…'

'I should have slammed the door in your face the first time I saw you.'

'Point being, you didn't… I didn't and we didn't,' he ground out harshly. 'I assumed you were protected; though, to be frank, I can't be sure if it would have made any difference.' His twisted smile held self-derision. 'When it comes down to it our carnal instincts can still master the most sophisticated of us when the attraction is as basic as it is between us. I should have checked to find out if you were pregnant. It was always a possibility.' He brushed back his hair in a distracted manner and frowned.

'It didn't seem fair to ask you to take responsibility…' she began, surprised by the self-recrimination in his manner. She felt she owed it to him to be as blunt as he was.

'Why, for God's sake?' he exploded. 'It's my fault!'

'We're almost total strangers…you despise me. How could I come to you and tell you I was pregnant and you were the father? I didn't think you'd believe me.'

'Is that really what you thought?'

'It's the truth, Callum,' she said quietly.

'The truth is, I don't know how I'd have reacted, but you didn't give me the opportunity to find out. You didn't give either of us the opportunity. I know you don't think much of me but surely you don't believe I wouldn't have accepted responsibility?'

'I didn't feel like being a complication in anyone's life. For me this baby isn't a complication, it's a blessing,' she said huskily. I don't want obligation, she wanted to shriek; I want love!

'What happened to your ambition?' he asked, watching her expressions with disturbing interest.

'I know you have me pegged as a devious tramp but if you'd ever bothered to ask I'd have told you my ambitions are no more than healthily normal. I'm certainly not prepared to sacrifice my personal life to achieve them.'

'Didn't you do just that when you lost your boyfriend to a more obliging female?'

'That,' she said firmly, 'was his problem, not mine.' She had gained a clearer perspective on that whole miserable affair lately. 'A husband who feels threatened by his wife's abilities,' she pondered thoughtfully, 'I can do without.'

'I just love your modesty,' Callum mused, leaning back in his chair and regarding her with narrow-eyed amusement.

'I was good at my job,' she protested. 'Even *you* have to admit that.'

'You have rare application,' he agreed readily. 'But Mallory's isn't the only place where your energies could be utilised.' Warm colour flooded her cheeks as she imagined what energies he was referring to. 'Next year,' he continued, 'we'll be launching our new wine label; I'll need someone to handle the promotion and marketing.'

'Is that a job offer?' she asked, trying to disguise from his astute gaze the embarrassing wrong turning her imagination had taken. The eloquent lift of one well-defined eyebrow made it clear that her slip had not gone unnoticed.

'What's wrong—don't you feel you're up to it?' he said sympathetically. 'I don't feel threatened by your abundant talent, if that's what you're worried about.'

'You've already sacked me once.'

'You resigned, as I recall, and when you were offered your old job you turned it down.'

'How would you know that?'

'Peter happened to mention it,' he said casually.

'In passing?' she suggested.

'I could have made a casual enquiry.'

The little shiver that traced a delicate pathway up her spine made her almost as flustered as his blue-eyed stare.

'If you want me to admit you made quite an impact on me I'm not going to deny it.'

'You're not? I d-did?' she stuttered hoarsely.

'It would be easier to come to terms with if I could believe you deliberately set out to seduce me, but I don't think you had any more control over what happened that night than I did. Did you make an impact?' he continued in a goaded voice, and she could see the vein in his temple throbbing. 'You were the embodiment of every erotic fantasy I've ever conceived.'

She swallowed convulsively as she listened to the rasp of his voice.

'You were warm and sensuous, Georgina. I should thank you for bringing me back to reality with a bump, waking up to find myself very alone the next morning. I might have made the same mistake my father did and confused lust for something else.'

'You were hardly a passive victim, Callum,' she responded shakily as she absorbed the implication of his last admission.

'I suppose under the circumstances you think you were the victim.'

'There's not much to be gained from allocating blame. We made a baby,' Georgina said quietly. 'I suppose that's all that really matters. If we hadn't I wouldn't be here, we wouldn't be together.'

'Why did you go to May, not me?'

The hard question threw her off balance. 'I didn't go to him, Callum. He just happened—'

'Never mind, it doesn't alter anything,' he interrupted tersely.

She stared in frustration at his closed expression and pushed away her plate. Sometimes, she mused angrily, he acted as if he was jealous, which was ridiculous.

*   *   *

The house was a sprawling converted farmhouse built of a rosy-hued stone. It was nestled on the lower slopes of a hillside above the fertile plains of a valley.

'You went out like a light,' Callum said as she rubbed her eyes and blinked around her. 'Slobbering all over my shoulder.'

'I do not slobber,' she contradicted him, recalling with a flush the muscled curve she had awoken against. 'Drool gently maybe…' she conceded, stretching luxuriously.

'It's not as remote as it seems,' Callum continued, helping her out of the passenger seat. 'The other approach road leads to a market town that's only a few kilometres away. My housekeeper, Mathilde, has agreed to move in, at least until after the baby is born, so you won't be alone. Her English is better than your French,' he added in a teasing tone.

'I've a jailer! How cosy,' she snapped, reluctantly accepting his help to lever herself from the vehicle. Right now it was winter but this was the sort of place that would have bougainvillea growing over the roof in summer; she liked it immediately. Will I still be here in the summer? she wondered.

If Georgina felt ungainly as she straightened up it was nothing to how she felt as a tall, slim shape emerged from the sprawling house and ran up the slight incline right into Callum's arms. She kissed him warmly on the lips and drew back, smiling. By the time the woman's eyes turned to her Georgina felt as unwieldy as the average tank.

'When did you breeze in, Josie?' Callum enquired, not seeming to find her form of greeting anything out of the ordinary. Georgina had ample opportunity to see that the young woman's profile was perfect.

'Last Saturday. Greg asked me to lend a hand as you were…delayed in London.' The willowy brunette flicked

Georgina a cold glance and turned her attention back to Callum.

'That was good of you, Josie. How's the weather been?' he asked, his eyes lifting to the dark clouds overhead.

'Cold enough to make me feel at home,' came back the laughing remark.

The wind was icy and Georgina was already aware of it cutting through the light fabric of her jacket. She certainly didn't feel at home; she felt like an intruder. 'I'll go in if you've no objection,' she said stiffly.

'Sorry, I haven't introduced you two. Georgina, this is Josie Dupont, my partner Greg's sister.'

Georgina responded to the slight inclination of the other girl's head in kind. She had to concede that the other girl was attractive, if you liked long-limbed, athletic creatures with madonna-like features. She was gloomily certain from his attitude that Callum did. Partner—she hadn't even known he had a partner, but then, she didn't know all that much about Callum, she reminded herself.

'Watch the cobbles outside the back door,' Callum yelled after her. 'They get slippery after rain.'

Georgina was panting when she stepped into the warmth of the large, flagstoned room and pushed the protective hood off her hair. As she shook the strands back the rich colour glowed in the subdued light; pregnancy had enhanced her crowning glory.

The kitchen ran the full width of the house. Its walls were exposed stone and the dark beams, from which drying herbs hung in bundles, were low. An ancient range stood in the inglenook, but, seeing the modern appliances in the room, she assumed its presence was more aesthetic than practical.

'Mathilde!' Callum yelled as he caught her up. 'You could have broken your neck out there,' he accused, cast-

ing Georgina an exasperated glance. 'Mathilde!' he said
again.

'Oh, Cal, I gave her the day off. Her niece was getting
married and she was desperate to go. I said you wouldn't
mind. Did I do wrong?' Josie asked, grimacing prettily as
she looked up at him.

'Of course not,' Callum said, the line of concentration
between his dark brows clearly revealing that he wasn't
happy with the situation. 'I need to catch up on things and
see Greg; he's been carrying my load long enough as it
is.'

I suppose that's my fault too, Georgina thought,
swamped by a sense of isolation. Why had she allowed
him to bring her here, take control of her life so completely? I must have been insane, she thought despairingly.

'What's stopping you?' the brunette asked.

'I can't leave Georgina alone.'

'Don't be ridiculous,' Georgina snapped, her colour
heightened as she intercepted the disdainful look the other
girl flicked her. 'Isn't the winery here?' she asked. She had
assumed the outbuildings she'd glimpsed housed it.

Josie gave a superior smile. 'No, it's the other side of
the valley,' she explained with a mix of superiority and
scorn that made Georgina's blood simmer. 'I'm sure Georgina understands you have other commitments, Callum.'

And are you one of them? Georgina wondered, watching
the way the girl smiled at Callum. Josie was cool, capable
and very easy on the eye—just the sort of female Callum
wouldn't mind hanging on his every word, she thought
sourly. She also had a waist, which was very tactless of
her!

'It's not open for discussion,' Callum said firmly. 'Tell
Greg to come over for dinner. You too, of course. We can
catch up then.'

Josie had to be satisfied with that and she hid her pique

well, but Georgina knew from the unfriendly glare she received that she was far from pleased with the outcome of this discussion. She'd wanted to whisk Callum away and she wasn't pleased at having her plans thwarted.

'I'll show you your room and you can rest,' Callum observed after the sounds of a four-wheel drive had disappeared into the distance.

'I don't need a keeper.'

'Opinion differs on that one,' he said drily. 'You do need a rest and if you weren't so stubborn you'd admit it.'

Common sense made her abandon her objections. A steep staircase led to the upper storey and Callum showed her into a large, airy room furnished mainly with antiques. The large bed had a brass frame and it was covered with a patchwork quilt. The flowers on the bureau made it seem possible that the absent Mathilde might be more welcoming than Josie; hopefully she wasn't in love with Callum too.

There seemed to be a rash of that particular disease at the moment, she thought, recalling the expression in Josie's grey eyes as she'd looked at Callum. If they'd had a relationship, or even *still* had a relationship, she thought with a swallow, no wonder the young woman viewed her with a lack of enthusiasm.

'It's very nice,' she said awkwardly. She turned to find Callum watching her with that curious intensity that was unique to him. She experienced the usual frisson of sensation that always occurred when she looked directly at him. It prickled along her senses like neat electricity. For a fleeting moment the awful sense of longing nearly swamped her. The effort to tear herself free of the hopeless yearning made her tremble. 'I am tired.'

Callum had looked as though he was about to say something but he pulled up short at her prosaic announcement and nodded curtly. 'If you need anything, just yell. There's a bathroom through that door,' he said, indicating the far end of the room.

Too tired to think, she kicked off her shoes and slid fully clothed beneath the bedcovers. Her dreams were dark, vivid and troubled...

She awoke with a start, sitting upright, confused and disorientated in a strange, darkened room. It took several heart-thudding moments before her temporary amnesia lifted.

It wasn't much more comforting to recall the truth; she was in some remote corner of the Languedoc with Callum, even though it was fairly obvious he wished her elsewhere. How much more cosy it would have been for him to return to find the lissom Josie on his doorstep.

If I hadn't been hanging around his neck like some sort of albatross he wouldn't have sent her packing, she thought bitterly. She spent a few agonising moments imagining what Callum and Josie would have been doing under different circumstances.

Always self-sufficient, it hurt Georgina to have her independence snatched away. It was made worse because Callum was the person she had become dependent on. His motivation was clear enough he felt the responsibility for the unborn child deeply. The fact that he was prepared to put up with her presence proved that.

She couldn't let herself grow used to being cherished and protected because the situation was a purely temporary one. How was she ever going to recover from this mindless infatuation when she was constantly seeing him? Infatuation! she thought with a grim smile. How like her to use euphemisms to hide from the truth, she thought with self-deprecating humour. All the associations, relationships and infatuations were not going to change the fact that she was in love with him!

She felt a movement in her belly and smiled, throwing

off her dark thoughts. Home was already growing cramped for the little one.

Exploring, she found the deep claw-footed bath a temptation. She turned on the taps and slowly slipped off her creased garments. Her reflection in the cheval-glass as she placed the bundle on the bed caught her eye. With fascination she looked at the swollen contours of her belly and the heavy ripeness of her breasts. The continual changes never failed to amaze her.

A movement on the periphery of her vision made her head turn as she gave a startled gasp. 'Callum!' Instinctively she snatched up her discarded shirt and held it in front of her.

She closed her eyes, imagining how gross and ugly he must find her body. She didn't want to look at him, sure that, at best, her own embarrassment must be mirrored in his eyes. She couldn't bear to see his repugnance.

'My God…' she heard him breathe.

Her eyes flickered open in protest as she felt the cotton shirt being firmly removed from her grip.

'You should be proud of the way you look, Georgina,' he said in a faintly unsteady voice that she hardly recognised.

She stood immobile as his hand tentatively touched the place where a waistline had once been. His expression was one of quiet awe and the touch of his long, sensitive fingers was gentle.

The glow of warm sensuality she felt surprised her. Confused and agitated, she wasn't sure she ought to feel like this in her present condition. But then why should being a mother stop her being a sensual person with healthy needs and appetites? Appetites that only Callum could excite.

She desperately wanted to step closer to him and increase the contact between them. 'I am proud,' she said as emotion rose to clog her throat. 'But I don't expect anyone else to share my fascination. I know I'm a bit of a blob.' She tried to smile to show she didn't mind if he thought that.

His blue eyes flickered to her face. 'You're beautiful, lush and ripe,' he said, his deep voice vibrantly caressing. 'I've never been this close to a miracle before.'

His response was too fervent to be a mere sop to her vanity. She gave a convulsive shiver and his expression changed to one of concern.

'You're cold,' he said, drawing a blanket off the bed.

'I was about to have a bath.'

'Come on, then; I'll help you. I don't want you falling; the sides are pretty steep.'

She didn't protest even though his reason sounded pretty thin; she might be a bit restricted but she could still climb in and out of a bath. It was a little like living out a part of her fantasy. A fantasy of having him close, cherishing her the way a lover—in the true sense of the word—would. If this child had been the result of a true, loving relationship this wouldn't be a fantasy, it would be real. Her starved senses had to be content with the illusion of intimacy.

Wordlessly he soaped her back and the heavy fullness of her breasts, his eyes examining the darkened aureoles of her nipples with open curiosity. Her body tingled from his gentle ministrations. He seemed fascinated by her body and she was content to watch the water slide off his sinewed forearms through half-closed eyes. She felt warm, relaxed and strangely at peace.

Later he joined her as she lay on the bed, and began to rub oil into the stretched skin of her abdomen. 'That's not too hard, is it?' he asked sharply as her back arched under his touch.

She turned her head on the pillow and he brushed aside

a strand of rich hair that fell across her flushed cheek. The action revealed the faint shadow of a bruise as she murmured a husky denial. He turned his head abruptly and she could sense his tension.

'This must be pretty boring for you,' she said apologetically.

'Boring?' he snarled, and she was shocked by the harshness in his voice. 'I'd hardly call it that. An exercise in self-restraint and a voyage of discovery is closer to the mark.' He took her chin between his thumb and forefinger and made her look him straight in the face. 'I'm trying not to think of making love to you, but it's hard. Very hard.'

She could hardly believe he meant it! He found her attractive...like this! The fierce light in his dense blue eyes and the compulsive way they ran over her body confirmed the admission that seemed to have been dragged from him against his will.

'You even smell more...female,' he rasped.

'I do?'

'You do.' A faint, half-mocking smile lifted the corners of his sensual mouth.

'Being pregnant makes some senses, like smell and taste, very acute. You smell awfully good,' she confided. 'And taste.' Her tongue flicked across her lips and her eyes fixed reflectively on the deep V of tanned skin that showed where his shirt was unbuttoned.

He caught his breath audibly and with a groan rolled to one side and sat upright. 'You have a good line in torture. Or had you forgotten what the doctor said?'

His words broke the sensual glow that had filled her. Mortified, she hurriedly pulled a sheet over her naked form. She had needed him to remind her! 'I'm sorry,' she whispered. Why wasn't she just content with being close? she wondered despairingly.

'I want this baby too and you mustn't worry that I'll do

anything to jeopardise that.' A faint flush highlighted the slanted line of his high cheekbones.

'It wasn't your fault. I... I...' She stumbled to say the right thing, then, unbidden, the last thing she intended to say fell from her lips. 'It seems like such a long time since anyone held me. God, *why* did I say that?' she wondered as tears welled in her eyes. 'It's all hormonal; I'm practically keeping the tissue companies in profit single-handed,' she wailed.

Callum had been about to say it probably wasn't such a good idea if he shared the same room and he wasn't sure he could cope with the constant temptation, when her outburst made him bite back the comment. He felt like all manner of selfish swine as she sobbed.

'I'll be around to hug you any time you want. I'm here to make sure you have a trouble-free pregnancy,' he joked, stroking her hair in a soothing fashion.

She looked at him with red-rimmed eyes. 'I wouldn't like to be an imposition.' She sniffed.

'God, I could shake you—' The sound of distant voices drifting up the stairs cut off his comment. Annoyance flashed across his face. 'I invited the Duponts to dinner,' he recalled, glancing at his wrist, but he'd left his watch in the bathroom. 'I didn't realise it was that time.' He leapt up and began straightening his shirt. 'Fortunately the cassoulet won't burn,' he observed, whipping an impatient hand through his hair.

'I'm not hungry,' she said, hating the idea of spending an evening with two total strangers, one of whom loathed her.

'I don't have time to subtly coax you, Georgina,' he said in an exasperated tone. 'Be down in fifteen minutes or I'll carry you down.'

She glared at the empty doorway, but she got up anyway. Knowing Callum, he was quite capable of fitting action to his words.

CHAPTER TEN

EXACTLY fifteen minutes later Georgina stood outside the kitchen doorway trying to compose her feelings. The wide-legged silky trousers had a tie waist that expanded to accommodate her bulk and she'd topped the green silk shirt with a long waistcoat. The light covering of make-up disguised the worst of the damage that her short emotional outburst had caused. Inside she was still writhing with discomfort at behaving like a clinging female. Callum might be the father of her child but she knew she had no real call on his loyalty.

She was actually about to step over the threshold when the words hit her.

'How does he know the baby is his? That's what I'd like to know. You know Callum and that moral streak of his. She's probably just an opportunist.'

'Josie!' came the hissed response. 'I hope you're not going to say anything like that in front of Callum.'

'Perhaps someone should.'

'Callum is more than capable of sorting out his own affairs,' came the dry, disembodied response.

'Did I hear my name being bandied around?'

Georgina felt a blast of cold air and heard the sound of the door closing. She realised her legs were trembling. I can't cope with this, she thought, swallowing the sour taste in her mouth. Then her pride came to her rescue. Why should I let that woman drive me away? she thought as revitalising temper whipped along her veins. Eyes sparkling with anger, she tossed her hair back and stepped into the room.

On the sofa covered with a vividly printed throw sat Josie and a man she assumed to be Greg. She only spared them a fleeting glance as her eyes were drawn automatically to Callum. He was standing beside the range, filling it from a basket of logs at his feet. He straightened up as she stalked in and regarded her quizzically. The room was warm from the heat thrown out by the cast-iron monster, but it had little to do with the colour in her cheeks.

She realised that everyone was staring at her expectantly. She had sailed in there full of righteous indignation, but what was she meant to do now? Clearly Callum hadn't heard the other girl's comments and even if he had he probably would only consider them reasonable observations from a friend with his best interests at heart. A friend who knew him better than she did. She suddenly felt extremely foolish standing there.

'You haven't met Greg yet, have you, Georgina?' Callum broke the lengthening pause.

There was none of the antagonism of his sister's expression in the face of the craggy-looking individual who rose to his feet with his hand extended. 'Nice to meet you, Georgina. I'd say Callum has told me a lot about you, but if you know Callum you'll know that would be a falsehood. Could teach clams a thing or two, could our Cal.' He sent his friend a swift grin. 'You look like you survived the journey pretty well. I hope you won't take offence if I say you give a new meaning to the word "glow."'

'She won't, but I might, Casanova,' Callum observed drily. 'Sit, Georgina. Remember what the doctor said don't stand if you can sit and don't sit if you can lie down.'

'Advice like that is what got her into this condition in the first place, isn't it?'

Josie's brother shot Josie a despairing look and smiled

apologetically at Georgina. He spread his hands in a con-
ciliatory gesture, clearly distancing himself from the catty
comment. Two spots of bright colour lit the brunette's
cheeks as she returned her brother's look with defiance,
but the quick glance she slid in Callum's direction was
clearly apprehensive.

'Sit here, Georgina.' He gently pushed her immobile
figure into a large armchair. It was impossible to tell from
his expression what he was thinking. 'Georgina didn't get
into *that condition*—' his lips moved in a *moue* of distaste
as he brushed the dust from the logs off his hands
'—alone,' he finished scathingly.

His blue eyes didn't soften as the other girl's lips quivered. The warning in his voice was impossible to miss. He
was staking his claim to the child very clearly and Georgina felt a spasm of alarm. Once it was born she might
very well be obsolete from his point of view. She couldn't
quell the uncomfortable speculation.

Georgina saw from the single glance she received from
Josie that she'd made an enemy. It wasn't a pleasant feeling!

Surprisingly the rest of the evening wasn't as awful as
it should have been. The undercurrents stayed under,
which was uncomfortable but not as bad as outright war-
fare.

'I didn't know you could cook,' Georgina observed as
Callum removed her plate and refilled her glass with min-
eral water. Everyone else was drinking wine.

'Good peasant stuff isn't beyond me, but I draw the line
at fancy sauces.'

'I didn't think anyone could cook on that antique,' she
replied huskily. He didn't smile naturally at her often, but
when he did—like now—the charismatic impact was
breathtaking.

'Don't let Mathilde hear you denigrate it; she refuses to have anything to do with the electric cooker.'

Anyone would have thought she'd be able to cope with this most unemotional of subjects, she thought despairingly. Why did she have this sudden overwhelming urge to weep? Just because there had been no suspicious shadows in his smile and she'd wished that it could always be that way. She turned her attention to Greg, hoping his calm, laid-back humour would help her regain her shredded composure. 'What part of America are you from?'

'Canada,' he corrected her with a laugh.

'Sorry. I'm not up to detecting regional variations,' she apologised with a smile.

'Our family are wine-makers too, and although Canadian wine has had an indifferent reputation up until recently we're in the middle of a renaissance.'

'And you're here missing it all,' she teased.

'Callum's enthusiasm can be contagious,' he responded, his eyes flicking an amused look in his friend's direction. 'Everyone said you couldn't make a top-class wine somewhere where the summers are hot and the winters cold but we did in Canada. This part of France has always produced wines, but not the really top-class stuff; Callum intends to change all that by bringing a little New World know-how to bear. As a French Canadian I found the challenge of getting back to my roots irresistible.'

'I'm sure Georgina's not interested in wine-making,' Josie put in with a superior smile.

'As a matter of fact I'd love to hear more. Callum's suggested I get involved with the marketing side of things next year,' Georgina contradicted her. 'Perhaps I could have a guided tour.' She smiled at Greg.

'I'll do that,' Callum said quickly.

'You'll be too busy being the little home-maker and

mother to give the sort of professional input we'll need. I'd hate to feel we made you neglect your responsibilities.'

'If I do decide to take this project on I'll fulfil my obligations,' Georgina responded.

'If I had a child I think I'd want to devote myself to doing that well before I started dabbling in other things.'

'I don't dabble.'

'Sorry, no offence intended,' Josie said with an apologetic smile that encompassed the silently observant Callum.

Like hell, Georgina thought, summoning a sickly-sweet smile.

'I'm sure Josie's only concerned that you don't overextend yourself,' Callum said.

'You made the offer,' she fired back indignantly. 'Or didn't you mean it?'

'I think it's a great idea,' Greg announced. 'Keep it in the family,' he continued, cheerfully oblivious to the embarrassment his observation had created.

'We've known Callum for years; Greg and I think of him as family. When did you meet him?' Josie asked.

'We met...at a wedding.' Callum threw Georgina a taunting look before he turned his attention back to their guests.

Georgina swallowed, hoping he wouldn't elaborate on this theme too fully. She shot him an apprehensive look from beneath the sweep of her lashes.

'Whose wedding?' Josie persisted in a disgruntled tone.

'My cousin's,' Georgina replied quietly. What had the girl expected to hear? That he'd picked her up in some bar? Josie would have a field-day if she knew how much more scandalous the innocent-sounding situation had been.

A violent clatter outside startled them all. 'What was that?' Georgina asked sharply.

'The wind here gets pretty violent sometimes,' Callum

said calmly, getting to his feet. 'It'll be that temporary roof
on the barn,' he said to Greg with a grimace. 'I meant to
secure it before the winter. We'd better see what the damage is.' He pulled a jacket down from the old-fashioned
coatstand by the door. 'No, Josie, you stay with Georgina,'
he said as the girl began to pull on her outer garment.

Josie's expression and the reluctance with which she
removed her coat revealed clearly that she didn't much
care for this instruction. 'I could help,' she muttered. The
scathing look she sent in Georgina's direction made it clear
that she despised anyone who wasn't equally physically
capable.

'Is it safe?' Georgina asked in a distracted voice. The
screeching wind sounded pretty ferocious to her.

'I'm touched by your concern.' Callum's contemplative
look made her raw nerve-endings scream.

'Wouldn't it be more sensible to wait until the wind
drops?' she persisted. She couldn't dispel the image in her
mind of Callum lying unconscious under the branches of
a fallen tree.

'Don't worry, Georgina; I'll put my foot down if the
man gets any heroic ideas.' Greg pulled his hat down
firmly over his ears and grinned.

She realised, a bit belatedly, that she'd done the concern
a little too thoroughly for comfort. 'I expect he can take
care of himself,' she mumbled distantly.

She froze with shock when Callum unexpectedly moved
to her side and kissed her very firmly full on the mouth.
The texture of his lips, the warmth and taste of him made
her knees grow weak and created a distant buzzing in her
ears. 'I can, but it's nice to have someone to worry about
me.' His eyes stayed briefly on her upturned face before
he turned abruptly and left.

Georgina felt the icy draught from the door that moved
the cups hooked on the large dresser but she was hardly

affected by the cold, warmed as she was by the glow his kiss had lit inside her.

'He doesn't love you, you know!'

The shrill words brought her rudely down to earth with a crash. Josie was pacing the floor, two bright patches of angry colour staining her cheeks. Her silence appeared to infuriate the girl further.

'He just feels responsible because of the baby. You've ruined his life,' she accused shrilly. 'You think you've been so clever, but before you trapped him we—' She bit back a choked sob of rage.

There wasn't much point in trying to reason with such passion, Georgina decided. She almost felt sorry for the young woman, who obviously found it impossible to disguise her feelings. Besides, what Josie had said was essentially true. She might not have deliberately set out to trap Callum, but the end result was much the same. Her heart twisted painfully in her breast as she strove to compose her feelings before speaking. Why are my hands so cold? she wondered, looking at her fingertips spread out on the table. She squeezed her fingers into fists and watched her knuckles grow white and bloodless.

'I didn't deliberately create this situation.'

'You could have got rid of it!' Josie yelled.

Georgina rose to her feet, quivering with a deep sense of outrage. 'I want this child and, whether you like it or not, so does Callum.' Her eyes swept disparagingly over the brunette's face.

'He doesn't want *you*.'

Georgina paled, aware that she couldn't deny this.

'I suppose the situation has a certain novelty value at the moment,' Josie continued, with a mocking laugh. 'If he wanted to play happy families with you surely he'd have married you? But Callum's too practical to tie himself down to some avaricious little tramp!'

Georgina placed her hands palm down on the table to support her weight. Her knees were shaking with reaction to the verbal onslaught. If he had loved her, or even if she hadn't loved him, the words would have glanced off her as the jealous, spiteful remarks that they were—but he didn't and she did! Each poisonous dart found its target.

The door hit the wall as the two men returned. Greg leant against it to close it against the wind. 'Get your coat on, Josie,' he said, panting from his exertions. 'I want to get back to the cottage before a tree or something blocks the road. It's rough out there tonight,' he observed, with almost British understatement.

And in here, Georgina thought, smothering a bubble of hysteria.

'Couldn't we stay here?'

Georgina hardly heard the brief argument that ensued between brother and sister. She couldn't take her eyes off Callum and the small, jagged tear in his cheek that oozed a trickle of blood. If he'd been badly injured or worse...! Devastation was just a thought away and she knew it— knew how much she needed him, how her life was inextricably linked with his. I can't tell him, ever! she thought.

Even if Josie wasn't the one, one day there *would* be a woman he loved and then what would become of her? Her feverish mind went up a gear as she imagined fierce custody battles. Could she cope with seeing her child accompany the man she loved and his partner for days out, let alone anything more permanent?

'You're hurt!' Josie cried, shrugging off her brother's restraining hand and rushing to Callum's side, dark, dramatic and beautiful.

'It's nothing, Josie,' Callum said, a shade of irritation in his voice.

Georgina could breathe now that his eyes had released

her own. It seemed sometimes as if he could see straight
into her soul.

'You ought to attend to it. Josie's right,' she said huskily. She wasn't going to offer. She'd never be able to
keep her hands from trembling, and breathing in his male
fragrance had a way of plunging her back into a state of
mindless oblivion. She had to maintain her defences. She
shook with the effort of remaining calm and passive.

'*I'll* do it,' Josie said scornfully, her voice implying that
any woman worthy of the name would be only too eager
to minister to her man. It was painfully obvious that she
was eager.

Callum took hold of her hands and firmly spun her
around in Greg's direction. 'Do as Greg says,' he said
abruptly in a tone that indicated that his patience was wearing thin. 'A tree has fallen through the barn and we've
made it as safe as possible. It would be stupid to hang
around.' He was the sort of man who made things happen
when he spoke; Georgina wasn't surprised to see their
guests leaving.

When they'd gone Georgina was still standing leaning
against the table. 'She's in love with you.'

'She *thinks* she is,' Callum corrected her calmly, lifting
his fingers experimentally to the cut on his cheek.

'And does she have reason to?'

'What is this, Georgina—an interrogation?' he asked,
his eyes narrowed. 'Would you mind if we were lovers?'
He seemed to be waiting tensely for her reply.

Georgina knew he was watching her, waiting for her
reaction, and she stayed as still as a statue. 'I don't care
who your lover is.' The lie fell readily from her stiff lips.
'Especially if it means I'm not pressurised.'

'When exactly did I pressurise you to be my lover?' His
voice was curiously flat. 'I hope you're not insinuating that
I'd force myself on you.'

'A peculiar sequence of events made us lovers, Callum. Nothing else.' She was painfully aware that force would never be a factor.

'You don't believe in Nemesis, then, Georgina?' He spoke with a curious inflection in his voice and a wild light in his blue eyes.

'I think she has a bizarre sense of humour if she exists,' she responded bitterly. 'Shall I help you with the clearing up?'

'Go to bed, Georgina,' he said with a hint of weariness in his deep voice. 'I won't inflict my company on you, if that's what's bothering you.'

Even though she was exhausted Georgina didn't sleep. She lay awake, her ears catching every creak and groan and old building made. Callum was true to his word and she didn't even hear him come upstairs.

CHAPTER ELEVEN

MATHILDE PROVED to be as protective as a mother hen. Her bullying wasn't subtle but it was well-meaning, and Georgina, who felt her girth increase in direct proportion to her exhaustion, was mostly happy to behave as the elderly Frenchwoman felt she ought.

During the weeks that followed Callum was as concerned for her welfare as ever, but since that first evening he had made no more intimate overtures. He was a polite and considerate stranger. It hurt as she watched the distance between them grow into a chasm as the weeks progressed. Knowing it was for the best made no difference to the bleakness she felt.

'I've prepared the room for the nurse,' Mathilde said, bustling into the kitchen, which was the hub of the house. 'We will have a full house once your mother is here next week. Will *monsieur* move into your room when she arrives?'

'I expect we'll manage somehow,' Georgina said faintly. She couldn't imagine he'd want to share a room with her and the baby, share the sleepless nights and all that went with them. She could just imagine the embarrassing comments her mother would make. Mathilde was bad enough! The new arrivals would give Callum all the less reason to be around, she thought bitterly.

She felt odd this morning; something was indefinably different. She'd spent a solid hour in the dressing room that Callum had transformed into a nursery for the baby, just pacing restlessly up and down. Callum had gone to so much trouble to make it perfect, with everything she could wish for for the new arrival—but it wasn't what she really wished for. If only the heart could be treated to a couple of coats of emulsion, she pondered ruefully. Another two weeks and the room would be occupied; despite the constant reminder she lived with, it didn't seem possible.

'I believe Monsieur Callum took Mademoiselle Josephine to dinner at Les Hirondelles last night,' Mathilde said, with a loud sniff of disapproval as she mentioned the local *auberge*.

'It was her birthday, Mathilde,' Georgina observed with a smile that was meant to indicate she hadn't a care in the world. 'I felt too tired to go.' Callum hadn't pushed the subject; he'd seemed almost relieved when she'd made her excuses.

'He wasn't back until late.'

'Wasn't he? I didn't notice,' she lied. She'd stayed awake until the small hours, listening for the sound of his footsteps. This morning he'd still been wearing last night's clothes and he'd avoided her eyes. She didn't need a picture to fill in the blanks!

'If the master shared your bed you'd notice.'

'Mathilde!' Georgina snapped, flushing.

The housekeeper lumbered off, still muttering direfully in her native tongue, and Georgina gave a sigh of relief. Callum had been spending less time at the house; sometimes it seemed as though he couldn't bear to be in her company. She'd caught a glimpse of Josie last night before they'd left, looking svelte and seductive in a low-cut black sheath. One look in her mirror told Georgina why he preferred the company of other women.

'*Madame.*'

Georgina rose from her chair awkwardly; the Frenchwoman insisted on the courtesy title and she'd stopped correcting her. 'What's wrong?'

'Gaston is here to take me to market and *monsieur* isn't back yet.'

Georgina frowned. Callum had promised to be back by the time Mathilde's nephew arrived to pick her up to do her weekly shop. 'Never mind; he won't be long.'

'*Monsieur* will be angry if I leave you alone, and the telephone here is still out of order.' The older woman was clearly torn. In the morning she shopped; in the afternoon she enjoyed catching up on gossip.

'*Monsieur* will be angry' indeed! Why were the world and his wife desperate to do exactly what Callum wanted? 'A few minutes alone won't make any difference,' Georgina insisted firmly. She was sick and tired of having him say what she could do, when she could do it, and for how long.

'You are sure? *Bien*.'

Seeing the housekeeper leave was a small victory in her continual bid to retain some freedom of action. Georgina had had so few private moments lately that she was relieved to have the place totally to herself. She found herself in the nursery, examining the tiny garments neatly stacked in the drawers. What was she going to do when the baby was born? She seemed incapable of thinking past that moment.

She couldn't stay with a man who needed other women to satisfy his sensual nature, certainly not when she loved the said man. Not even for the child. Would he try and prevent her going? She sighed; her thoughts seemed stuck in a constant groove with no outright solution.

She was still sitting on the floor, her back against the gaily decorated wall, when she realised the nagging backache she'd had since the previous evening was more than that. The pain started low in her thighs and rose upwards in a wave of pressure.

It can't be, she thought, shaking her head and dismissing the idea; I've got two weeks to go yet. All the same she glanced at the clock suspended above the cot. The painted illustrations from a nursery rhyme seemed to mock her.

An hour later and after a rushed trip to the bathroom she knew it was the real thing. She spoke out loud to still the rising panic that threatened to swamp her. She was excited and afraid.

'Callum will be back soon. Everyone knows the first one takes hours and hours. Ugh!' She grabbed onto a bureau for support. It seemed advisable under the circumstances to take to her bed. She tried the telephone extension but it was still dead. 'I will not panic,' she said. Her defiant voice sounded abnormally loud in the room. A strange calm descended over her as a pattern of pain and rest established itself.

A knock—soft, then louder—heralded company. How long had she lain there? She didn't know; time had little meaning.

'Georgina!'

She heard the door creak then Callum's soft footfalls on the carpet. 'Where's Mathilde?'

Georgina opened her eyes. 'She went with Gaston.'

'She should have waited until I got back,' he said, his face harsh with irritation. 'Can I get you anything?'

'A doctor might be good. I think it's too late for an ambulance.' As if to illustrate this point she grabbed hold of the metal bed-frame as she felt another wave of pain wash over her.

'You're not saying…? You can't; it's not time yet. Georgina!' She heard the panic in his voice—panic she'd never heard before. 'I'll get the car.' This time his voice was firmer, more in control, and she opened her eyes.

'It's too late for that, Callum. He's going to come *now*!'
Another contraction hit her and a cry was ripped from her
throat. The sound, eerie and primitive, somehow shocked
him into action.

'That's it, sweetheart; it's all right. I'm here now.'

Gasping, she relaxed onto the pillows whilst her body
had a temporary respite from its labours. 'You took your
time,' she said as he wiped the beads of sweat from her
forehead. 'I wanted you!' she wailed.

A fierce light flared in his eyes. 'Don't worry. I've done
this loads of times before.'

She stared at him with red-rimmed eyes. 'You have?'

'Cattle, sheep. Can women be *that* different?'

Her laughter was cut off by the urge to push hard and
her face creased with effort.

His hands weren't shaking as he gently examined her;
this fact alone amazed him. Over the past month or so
he'd read enough to know theoretically what should happen, but he knew that theory and practice were rarely the
same thing. He found he was praying swiftly and fervently
in his head, promising anything if only this would go
smoothly. The responsibility for two lives was in his
hands; the knowledge lay heavily. Seeing Georgina's pain
and knowing there was nothing he could do to alleviate it
filled him with the most awful sense of helplessness he'd
ever experienced.

She'd got this far all alone while he'd been deliberately
staying away. His anger turned inwards, burning hot and
unforgiving. If anything happened to her…to the baby…
he'd carry it with him for the rest of his days. Then as she
called his name he had to put the anger aside and spoke
soothingly, with an authority he didn't feel.

'Georgina, the head's coming.' He took her hand and
guided it to the crowning skull of the unborn child. His
face was wildly exultant, tense with strain and wet with a

sheen of sweat. 'Just a couple more pushes, sweetheart. You're doing so well.'

He didn't believe what he'd said was true until it happened and the child slithered out into his waiting hands. 'We've got a daughter and she's perfect!' His voice rang with joy. The cry as the baby's throat cleared made his eyes mist over with emotion.

Child against her breast, Georgina felt swamped by a surge of sheer exhilaration. 'We did it; we did it,' she kept breathing, touching the tiny fingers, awed by the miracle of new life in her arms.

'*You* did it,' Callum corrected her, his eyes full of the solemnity of the occasion. He knew enough basic midwifery to clamp the cord, and, standing back, his whole body shaking with reaction, he watched the child—his child—*their* child, perfect and beautiful—suckle at her mother's breast.

An hour later Mathilde returned. She opened the door and gasped, her eyes nearly popping out of her head. 'Gaston!' she screeched. '*Le docteur...*'

'It's a bit late for that, Mathilde,' Georgina observed complacently, staring at her new daughter, her face alight with love.

'Get him all the same, Mathilde,' Callum said, getting up from the side of the bed.

'I don't have to go to hospital, do I?'

'Shall we let the doctor decide that?'

Unable to tear her eyes from the delicate features of the sleeping child, she nodded. 'She is beautiful, isn't she?'

'Exquisite,' he said huskily. 'Can...can I hold her?'

She looked up; he'd sounded almost defensive about the request, and then she saw in his eyes the suspicion that she'd deny him the appeal. 'Of course you can, Callum,' she said emotionally. 'She's your daughter. I don't know what I'd have done if you hadn't come.'

Some of the tension disappeared from his shoulders as he took the firmly wrapped bundle from her hands. 'I expect you'd have managed.'

A certain quality in his searching regard of the tiny face made her heart ache. He looked so proud, so stunned still by this new life he'd helped bring into the world. She knew she couldn't deprive him of this child—part of him—part of them; it would be wrong.

'You knew she'd be a girl. Have you thought of any names?' she asked impulsively.

'Are you asking my opinion?' He knew that this concession was part of a bigger decision she'd just made and his grave expression was appreciative of the fact. 'I like Rachel.'

'Rachel Campion...mmm... I like it.'

'Rachel Stewart?'

She shot him a startled look.

'Don't say anything now, but think about it,' he said quietly, almost as if he was regretting his impulsive words. 'You must be tired.'

'For the baby...for Rachel?' she asked, her throat aching with unshed tears.

'She needs us both.'

Georgina watched the movement of his throat muscles, her mind spinning. She had moral blackmail and practicality when she wanted love and passion. For a while there everything had seemed so perfect, two people sharing the ultimate creation of that love, but she'd only been seeing what she wanted to see. Baby Rachel wouldn't change the way Callum felt about her any more than she would change how she, Georgina, felt about him. He was asking her to make the same concessions that he was willing to make. Could she refuse the request even if it hurt?

The strident sound that emerged from the small bundle distracted them both. Handing the child back to her, Callum watched in fascination as the infant fastened onto her mother's breast with single-minded ferocity.

Callum sat in the chair beside the bed and watched them. If Georgina had let her attention wander she'd have seen the restless, hungry expression in his eyes. When Callum got up to leave she didn't notice. After being so involved he felt curiously redundant to the whole process. He roused himself from his introspective mood and set about coping with the practicalities. There were people to inform and a telephone to get reconnected in a hurry.

'Are you trying to drive that man away?' Lydia demanded, running her daughter to ground in the kitchen.

'Mother, I'm tired, so if you want a fight couldn't it wait until later?' Georgina faced her angry parent with an expression of resignation. Lydia had come to stay shortly after Rachel's birth six weeks before and the situation was already becoming untenable. She ought to be grateful— she was grateful—but Lydia was openly disapproving of her relationship with Callum and wasn't afraid of voicing her disgust.

'Are you happy that he's chasing around the countryside with that...female?'

'My happiness is neither here nor there,' Georgina snapped. 'I haven't got any monopoly on his time. Callum is here to help with Rachel when I need him.'

'And is that enough?' her mother asked.

'It'll have to be,' Georgina said dispiritedly.

Lydia's expression softened but she pursued her topic with typical exhausting single-minded determination. 'Doesn't it occur to you you could be a little more... welcoming to him?'

'What do you suggest?' Georgina asked with exasperation. Did her mother really think she needed the inadequacies of her situation pointed out? 'I do the Dance of the Seven Veils on the kitchen table?'

'If it works why not give it a whirl?'

'Mother!'

'Well, you could take a little more trouble with the way you look.'

'Thanks for the moral support, Mother.'

'I've no patience with this stiff-necked attitude of yours, Georgina. If you want the man what's so wrong about showing him?' Her daughter was flushed-cheeked and thoughtful as she left the room. 'You do want Callum, don't you?'

'How long is Mother staying?' Georgina asked later when Callum returned. 'She's driving me insane! I know I sound an ungrateful wretch,' she said ruefully as Callum gave her a quizzical look.

'Here, have some.' He uncorked a bottle of wine and half filled a glass.

'Should I?' she asked dubiously.

'Half a glass of wine won't harm Rachel. It'll do her far more harm if her mother is ready to climb up the walls at three in the morning,' he observed sensibly. 'You have to relax while you can.'

Georgina nodded and sipped the rich, ruby-coloured liquid. 'I never thought it would be this tiring,' she admitted. God, Mother was right—I do look a wreck, she thought gloomily.

'It's early days yet.' He pulled up a chair and sat astride it, resting his hands on the backrest. 'You should go and get some sleep,' he observed, examining her pale face. 'If Lydia wakes Rachel up again I'll strangle her and bury her at the bottom of the garden,' he offered generously. 'Lydia, that is—not Rachel.'

This drew a laugh from her. 'I expect I'm overreacting,

but nothing I'm doing is right, according to Mother,' she said with frustration.

'Her mother probably did the same to her,' he said calmly. 'Call it continuity.'

Georgina regarded him with wonder through the swirling liquid in her glass. His calmness constantly amazed her; nothing seemed to throw him—not her tearful outbursts or the baby crying at two in the morning.

'I'm not sure I could have coped without you,' she said huskily. Her words drew his sharp gaze to her face. 'I'm lucky.'

'That's an astounding thing to hear you say,' he observed, his expression more cautious than amazed.

'Mother was asking what our plans are.'

'And what did you tell her?' he asked, a spasmodic clenching of a muscle along his jaw belying his casual tone.

'I said I couldn't think beyond the moment.' She watched apprehensively as his jaw tightened and his lips thinned.

'I see...'

'But I can see we have to sort things out. We can't drift like this for ever. It wouldn't be fair—to either of us.'

'I asked you to marry me.'

'I suppose you did, after a fashion,' she agreed, her heart thudding as she picked her words with painful care. 'It was a very emotional moment. I thought you might change your mind.'

'That won't happen,' he said in a clipped tone.

'It would be easy for me to say yes for all the wrong reasons. Can't you see that?' she pleaded.

'I see you want to keep your options open.'

'What do you mean?'

'I mean now you have had Rachel there's nothing stopping you taking up where you left off with May.' He was watching her with a curious intensity.

The completely unreasonable nature of his accusation roused her temper. 'You've got some nerve after spending the night with Josie the day before Rachel was born!' She tried not to remember his absence but the memory was always there, nagging at her in contented moments.

He looked totally blank for a moment, then a faint flush mounted his cheekbones. 'That seems like a lifetime ago,' he observed drily.

He didn't even bother defending himself, she thought, stilling her quivering lower lip with a sharp nip of her teeth. You're doing well, Georgina, she told herself. Don't cry now, she thought, gulping back a sob. Don't let him see you care.

'If I told you I'd be faithful once we were married…' Once more his eyes avoided her face, almost as if he was embarrassed.

'I'd laugh,' she said stiffly, with a toss of her head.

Her sarcasm made his eyes flash and his big, powerful body grow taut. 'Why didn't you tell me that you were at Mallory's that day to meet Mary, not May?'

The unexpectedness of this question left her staring as the blood drained dramatically from her face. 'How did you…?'

'I had a very interesting conversation with Mary when she phoned just after Rachel was born. She was relieved everything had gone well; she felt responsible for being late that day.'

He'd known that long! Georgina stared at him, trying to read his expression. 'Why didn't you mention it?'

'More to the point, why didn't you?' he parried. 'I should have killed the bastard,' he reflected harshly, his fists clenching as he seemed overcome by a sudden spurt of violent anger. 'When I think what he could have done.'

'He made a few heavy passes at me,' Georgina confessed, attempting to sound casual. 'I handled them clumsily. I never—'

'Your sexual experience before me consisted of a few clumsy attempts with Alex, didn't it, Georgina?'

She gave a weak smile. 'Two, if you're counting,' she admitted, recalling the miserable, inhibited occasions.

His eyes closed on a jagged sigh and he shook his head. 'Couldn't you have told me that?' The words exploded from him as his eyes snapped open.

'As a matter of fact, no, I couldn't. You didn't want to hear and I had no reason to imagine you'd be interested.'

He went pale but the ruthless glow in his blue eyes didn't fade. 'I said some pretty vile things to you,' he said from between clenched teeth.

'I can hear Rachel,' Georgina said, her maternal antennae picking up the faint sounds of their child's hungry cries. 'I've got to go.'

Her daughter's immediate needs left Georgina little time to brood. Callum hadn't tried to stop her going; he'd just stood there with a peculiar, agonised expression on his face. He eventually walked in when she had just lain the small bundle back in her cradle.

Georgina straightened up and put her finger to her lips.

'Come on through; we need to talk,' he said tersely. The movement of his eyes made her aware that she hadn't adjusted her clothes after feeding the baby. Fumbling with the buttons of her shirt, she followed him into the adjoining room.

'Isn't it a bit late to hide your body from me, Georgina?' he said drily, his eyes on the creamy upper slopes of her generous breasts.

She paused, her clumsy fingers reluctantly falling away from their half-finished task. 'When you put it that way, I suppose it is,' she agreed bleakly.

'You're right—things can't go on like this.'

She had known this moment would come; he'd had enough, but steeling herself to hear him say so was the hardest thing she'd ever done.

'I'm sure we can come to some sort of civilised arrangement.'

'Civilised!' he growled in a tone that made her jump. 'Who wants civilised?'

'Why, you do, don't you? I've heard your idea of the perfect marriage and it wouldn't do for me.'

'This should be the best time of our lives, Georgina. Tell me what would do for you.'

A solitary tear escaped and trickled slowly down her cheek. She was crying for what might have been.

'Tell me what you want,' he persisted rawly, his eyes riveted to the spot of moisture.

'I want you and Rachel.' She gritted her teeth and raised her clenched fists to her mouth as the forbidden truth escaped. 'No, no—just pretend I didn't say that.' She half turned away but he caught her shoulder and swung her roughly around to face him.

'Say it again!' he demanded.

She made an ineffectual attempt to pull away. 'Don't make this worse for me than it already is, Callum,' she pleaded.

'Worse for you? Have you any idea what sort of hell it's been for me?' The jerk of his head indicated the brass-framed bed. 'Every night, not able to touch you—' He broke off, his voice suspended by the pain that contorted his face. 'Damn it, woman. Don't tease me with statements like that and turn away.' His hands tightened on her shoulders.

'I'm not teasing you, Callum,' she protested, shocked by his response. 'I'm sorry, but I fell in love with you. Do you see now why I couldn't possibly marry you?'

He went stock-still and she could feel a shudder gather strength and run along his taut frame. 'I might be dense,' he said slowly in the strangest tone she'd ever heard, 'but no, I don't see. Perhaps you should explain.'

'I can't be pragmatic and sensible,' she shouted, her eyes dark with anguish. 'I'd be jealous and...I wouldn't be the sort of wife you want at all.'

'You mean the idea of me with another woman would drive you wild?' he suggested. 'That you'd respond irrationally? Like I did when I thought of you with Simon May—or, for that matter, with anyone else but me?'

She blinked rapidly and succeeded in catapulting one of her contact lenses out. 'Oh, no!' she groaned in frustration. What brilliant timing! 'Not now.'

'What's wrong?'

'I've lost one of my lenses,' she wailed, feeling against the nearest solid surface, which happened to be his chest, to find the offending item. 'I can't see a thing.'

'I don't mind you feeling your way,' he said softly, pressing one of her hands harder against the surface of his stomach. The delicious contraction of muscles under her fingertips made her gasp gently and raise her myopic wide eyes to his face. That he found her exploration arousing was evident as he pressed closer to her, making her insides melt.

She licked her dry lips. 'Is this the right time to say I love you?' she asked tentatively, giving her lens up for lost. She was never one to shirk a challenge, especially one with the sort of rewards this particular task could yield.

'Absolutely the right time,' he growled, a fierce blaze of triumph in his eyes.

The kiss went on a long time as he plundered the moistness of her mouth. His hands moved in her hair and a series of fierce, hungry moans erupted from his throat.

When he lifted his head she stared at him in dazed submission.

'I don't believe this,' she whispered hoarsely. 'You hate me.'

He grinned. 'If only life were that simple, my lovely Georgina,' he teased, running a finger around the firm curve of her chin and taking it firmly in the palm of his hand.

Georgina gave a shuddering sigh and smiled. It wasn't exactly an avowal of eternal love but she felt extremely optimistic.

The smile had a visibly powerful effect on Callum, who caught his breath in a series of hoarse gasps. 'One smile like that and I'd never have lasted these past weeks,' he admitted. Whilst he spoke one hand was peeling back the half-fastened sides of her shirt. He proceeded to flick the front fastener of her bra undone. He swallowed as the creamy fullness of her breasts escaped. 'Sweet mercy,' he breathed. 'Can I touch? Or are you too tender?' he asked, drinking in the sweet fragrance of her hair.

'Sensitive, but not tender now,' she said softly as he sucked the tips of the fingers she placed against his mouth. 'Could you explain how this is happening, Callum?' she asked dreamily.

'I didn't want to come to London or get involved in the internal wrangling of that bloody agency, and most of all I didn't want to fall in love with a wicked, red-haired witch in a silly hat.'

She couldn't stop smiling. 'It was a very expensive hat.'

'I have built-in prejudice when it comes to phrases like love at first sight.' He shrugged self-consciously. 'You know my history. You hit me for six, woman, and I came up fighting,' he growled. 'I'd seen firsthand what blind infatuation could do; I'd always been determined never to place myself in that situation and become a victim of my own desire. Then that night in that damned awful hotel I fell at the first blow. I didn't even put up a fight.'

'Kiss,' she corrected him happily. 'First kiss.' I'm really enjoying this story, she thought, giving a small, ecstatic sigh.

'My first thought when I woke was how was I going to get you to accept I'd been in your bed under false pretences. I'd been too jet-lagged to stay conscious the night before and tell you I was the dreaded nephew. As it happened, that wasn't a problem, as you weren't in the bed, or the room, or the hotel,' he recalled grimly.

'I thought you'd be relieved that I'd gone,' she said anxiously. 'I knew I couldn't act as if it meant nothing to me so it seemed sensible to...'

'Run away.'

She nodded guiltily, wondering how differently the last few months might have turned out if she'd stayed. 'I thought you'd cringe if I was there the next morning gushing about how marvellous it was.'

'I thrive on a moderate amount of gushing.'

'You *were* hateful to me,' she reminded him.

'Too right!' he said, his eyes gleaming. 'I'd been stupid enough to break all my own rules and fall for a scheming, sexy body and a pair of innocent eyes. I wanted to believe every rotten thing I could about you. I wanted to see you crawl. I sort of liked it when you didn't,' he admitted, stroking the receptive peak of one breast, cupping her flesh and sighing with hoarse delight as it overflowed from his hand. 'I liked lots of things about you.'

'You hid it well,' she told him teasingly. Her head dropped against his chest as her knees sagged; the relief and joy of the occasion was taking a physical toll. 'I was pretty miserable too, if that helps. I was so scared when I first realised I was pregnant.'

'It doesn't help at all,' he said hoarsely. 'When I think of you—alone, carrying our baby,' he groaned.

'I wanted to tell you,' she confided, burying her face in his shoulder. 'But I thought you'd think it was just another of my devious schemes. I was sure that even if you accepted the situation it would only be out of a sense of responsibility. I didn't want your obligation, Callum, I wanted your love,' she revealed huskily.

'I suppose I can't blame you for thinking I'd reject you,' he said, his voice anguished. 'I wanted to kill May when I thought the baby was his. And when I knew she was mine I...I hated myself for letting you go through all that alone.'

'You can't blame yourself,' she protested.

He gazed fondly into her indignant face and laughed. 'I could get used to having you in my corner,' he confessed.

'It's somewhere I didn't think you wanted me to be. You were always with Josie.'

'Inevitably I was some of the time,' he agreed, rubbing the side of her nose with his thumb and gazing at her upturned face tenderly. 'But not as much as I let you think. Incidentally, I didn't string Josie along; I told her I'm in love with you. I did think a bit of healthy jealousy might be justified, considering the urgency of my need.'

'You heartless rat,' she said with mock severity. The blaze in his eyes recompensed her for the anguish she had suffered.

He grinned wickedly. 'The night before Rachel was born I was out driving all night. I parked in some God-forsaken spot. I couldn't trust myself not to touch you when we were together and you'd made it pretty clear you didn't want me to. I thought it might get easier after the baby was born but it's got gradually worse; you've been pushing me further away!' He tilted her chin up and looked reproachfully into her eyes.

'I thought it was Rachel you wanted, not me. I needed you to love *me*.'

He gave a brilliant, savage grin. 'It's ironic when you think about it. We've both been immersed in our separate cells of self-induced solitude. If we'd actually said what we were feeling we could have saved ourselves months of misery. I wanted to confront you with the Simon May thing as soon as Mary let the truth slip but you were so wrapped up in our daughter I was going to wait until you weren't so exhausted.'

'When will that be, do you suppose—eighteen years' time?'

'I've heard that's when the trouble starts,' Callum said solemnly.

'About the legacy from Oliver,' Georgina said, trying hard not to be distracted by the erotic movements of his hands over her body from explaining the one major obstacle that stood between them.

'What about it?' he said, reluctantly raising his head when she repeated herself nervously.

'You don't sound very interested,' she said a shade indignantly.

'It's a long time since I could convince myself you were an avaricious little go-getter. The fact that I knew you must have overcome strong moral objections to sleep with me that night convinced me that you felt a strong sexual attraction at least. I'm sure Oliver had his own obscure reasons for giving you the money, but I'm not losing any sleep over them. Convincing you you need me as much as I do you has occupied most of my thoughts recently,' he confessed bluntly.

'He was an old flame of Mother's before and after she was married. He also tried to make her leave my father and contributed to the eventual breakup of their marriage. I think the money was his way of making amends.'

'Terminally selfish old devil,' Callum muttered angrily. 'I should warn you to expect more of the same when my mother grants you an audience. I can't wait to show you off to everyone at Wollundra, and Rachel can meet her new cousin.' Tricia had produced a son eight weeks before Rachel was born.

'It was very nice of your mother to send us a congratulations card,' Georgina said tentatively; she knew that she had to tread carefully where Callum's relationship with his mother was concerned.

'It'll kill her to admit she's a grandmother,' he laughed. 'Don't look so solemn,' he admonished her. 'I stopped letting my mother's shortcomings affect my life the moment I fell in love with you, my darling. You were and are a sweet revelation. The more I tried to put you out of my mind, the worse it became. I hope you don't mind that we put the cart before the horse a little, having Rachel before the wedding?'

'Aren't you being a mite premature?' she teased happily. Did life get any better than this? she wondered, her heart soaring.

'I've been incredibly patient, woman, and don't expect it to continue!' he warned, kissing her parted lips. 'You'll marry me.'

'I'm not sure it's a good idea for us to work together as well as being married—if the offer still stands?' she quizzed mischievously.

'I seem to recall you saying you wouldn't work *for* me but would deign to work *with* me. That arrangement sounds pretty good to me. Just say when you feel ready and we'll organise things with Rachel. I have a very flexible maternity policy.'

'You mentioned patience,' she said, a smile curving her lush mouth.

'Uh-huh,' he said huskily, and she could feel his body throbbing.

'I'm feeling a little impatient myself.' She looked up at him with half-closed eyes, her lashes casting a shadow over the high curve of her cheekbones.

'Parents should take any opportunity for rest and relaxation they can. I read that somewhere.'

'Sounds like good advice. I don't mean to sound pushy but babies don't sleep for long—at least, ours doesn't.'

'Wanton hussy,' he said, sweeping her up in his arms and laying her across the bed.

'I could learn to be,' she said as he joined her. 'With a little assistance.'

Callum, she learnt, could be very generous with his guidance...

If you enjoyed what you just read,
then we've got an offer you can't resist!

Take 2 bestselling love stories FREE!
Plus get a FREE surprise gift!

 **HARLEQUIN®**
Makes any time special ™

 WIN A DREAM

In celebration of Harlequin®'s golden anniversary

Enter to win a *dream!* You could win:

- A luxurious trip for two to
  The Renaissance Cottonwoods Resort
  in Scottsdale, Arizona, or

- A bouquet of flowers once a week for a year
  from **FTD**, or

- A $500 shopping spree, or

- A fabulous bath & body gift basket, including
  K-tel's *Candlelight and Romance* 5-CD set.

Look for **WIN A DREAM** flash on
specially marked Harlequin® titles by
Penny Jordan, Dallas Schulze,
Anne Stuart and Kristine Rolofson
in October 1999*.

FTD

RENAISSANCE.
COTTONWOODS RESORT
SCOTTSDALE, ARIZONA

K-TEL

HARLEQUIN PRESENTS®

*invites you to see
how the other half marry in:*

SOCIETY WEDDINGS

This sensational new five-book miniseries invites
you to be our VIP guest at some of the most talked-
about weddings of the decade—spectacular events
where the cream of society gather to celebrate the
marriages of dazzling brides and grooms in
breathtaking, international locations.

Be there to toast each of the happy couples:

Aug. 1999—**The Wedding-Night Affair**, #2044,
Miranda Lee

Sept. 1999—**The Impatient Groom**, #2054,
Sara Wood

Oct. 1999—**The Mistress Bride**, #2056,
Michelle Reid

Nov. 1999—**The Society Groom**, #2066,
Mary Lyons

Dec. 1999—**A Convenient Bridegroom**, #2067,
Helen Bianchin

Available wherever Harlequin books are sold.

HARLEQUIN®
Makes any time special ™

"Don't miss this, it's a keeper!"
—Muriel Jensen

"Entertaining, exciting and
utterly enticing!"
—Susan Mallery

"Engaging, sexy...a fun-filled romp."
—Vicki Lewis Thompson

See what all your favorite authors
are talking about.

Coming October 1999 to a retail store near you.

Coming Next Month

HARLEQUIN PRESENTS®

THE BEST HAS JUST GOTTEN BETTER!

#2055 THE BABY GAMBIT Anne Mather
Matteo di Falco was falling in love with Grace Horton. But it was Grace's friend who was determined to marry him, by any means necessary. Matteo was used to getting what he wanted, and this time he wanted Grace—not her friend!

#2056 THE MISTRESS BRIDE Michelle Reid
(Society Weddings)
The high-profile affair between Sheikh Raschid Al Kadah and Evie Delahaye was in the media spotlight because their families were determined to keep them apart. Then Evie discovered why she *must* marry Raschid....

#2057 HAVING HIS BABIES Lindsay Armstrong
(Expecting!)
Clare had independence, a thriving law firm and a wonderful lover in Lachlan Hewitt. She knew she loved him, but she didn't know how he really felt. Then she discovered she was pregnant. What on earth would Lachlan say?

#2058 MARRIAGE UNDER SUSPICION Sara Craven
The anonymous note suggested that Kate's husband, Ryan, had betrayed her. Kate was determined to keep her man. But while their marriage was in jeopardy, there was no way she'd tell Ryan she was expecting his baby!

#2059 AN ENGAGEMENT OF CONVENIENCE Catherine George
Leo Fortinari seemed to be fooled by Harriet's impersonation of her friend, Rosa. He'd even agreed to a pretend engagement with Harriet. But Leo knew that the woman in his bed wasn't Rosa—for the impostor was a virgin!

#2060 GIBSON'S GIRL Anne McAllister
Chloe's boss, Gibson Walker, was sinfully gorgeous, but Chloe had to resist him—she was engaged to someone else! But the more she ignored him, the more he wanted her. And soon it became a question of who was seducing whom....